NEVER EVER LEAVE ME

ELLY GRANT

CHAPTER ONE

Katy heard the slap, a muffled thud against her ear, a split second before she felt the sharp sting on her cheek. Her eye blurred as it watered, running tears down the side of her nose. The impact knocked her head round and for a moment she felt disorientated. She staggered, slightly off balance, but managed to stop herself from actually falling, instead she grabbed the edge of the sink to steady herself.

"Do you think I want to be out of work, you stupid bitch? Do you think I want to be down at the pub drinking with those losers?"

Katy cowered, her hand holding her cheek where Gordon had hit her. She was shaking with shock.

"Cat got your tongue? Nothing smart to say? Now there's a change."

Gordon reeled away from her towards the kitchen door. As he manoeuvred past the table, he swept the stack of newly dried crockery onto the floor then kicked at the debris sending shards of broken china across the room. Katy exhaled her bated breath and began to cry. She was scared. The man she loved, the man she'd married only six months before had changed beyond all recognition. Gordon blamed everything on losing his job, but it was his fault he was fired. He was always a smartass, always thought he could get away with anything. He assumed the manager was stupid and wouldn't figure out who was stealing the stock. Katy had tried to warn him.

"We don't need the money," she'd said. "We're both working and we're doing okay. Surely it's not worth the risk."

"Everyone needs a bit extra," he'd replied. "Besides, I won't get caught. That old duffer will think the customers are stealing the stuff. He'll never know it's me."

But Gordon was caught, and he was lucky just to be fired and not charged. That incident happened three months ago. The day before Katy found out she was pregnant. If he'd appeared in court, he'd have had some explaining to do as she had no knowledge of his previous record. Now, understandably, nobody would employ him. Living in a small town the word went round quickly.

He was rather controlling even before they were married. Powerfully built, sex with Gordon was all about him, but Katy had never had a lover before and mistook his roughness for passion. She expected nothing and therefore wasn't disappointed. Her own father had been a cold and distant man, so any attention was welcome.

Annie, Gordon's sister, tried to warn her. "He's just like my dad," she'd said on more than one occasion. "My dad is a violent drunk, but my mum always takes him back."

"Gordon isn't like him," Katy protested. "He loves me and we're going to have a good life together. Besides, I'm not like your mum. A man would only have to lift his hand to me once, and I'd be out of the door."

She could visualise Annie's pursed lips, the shake of her head, her despairing look. The bruise forming on her cheekbone clear evidence that Annie was right. She stood motionless, listening fearfully, trying to determine where in the flat Gordon was and, more importantly, if he was returning to the kitchen. An involuntary shudder ran down her spine. 'Aye, aye, lass, someone's just walked on your grave', her mother's old saying popped into her head and she shuddered again. Her instinct was to run, but Gordon might try to stop her, he might hit her again and where could she run to? Her shoes were in the bedroom, her handbag in the sitting room, a suitcase to pack her clothes was in the cupboard in the hall. She strained to listen again then she heard the bathroom door close and the lock turn.

Suddenly, she was moving like lightning. She raced into the sitting room and grabbed her handbag then practically flew into the bedroom where she stepped into her shoes before grabbing a neatly ironed duvet cover from the pile of fresh laundry on the blanket box. She stood still and listened again, to her relief she could hear the shower running. Not wasting a moment, she grabbed clothes from the wardrobe and underwear from the drawer then she stuffed everything unceremoniously into the pocket of the duvet. She added to this the biscuit tin containing her important and precious items which she'd kept at the bottom of the wardrobe then ran for the door.

Passing the bathroom, she heard the shower stop flowing and for a moment she panicked. Should she go or should she run back to the bedroom? Another shudder rippled down her spine and the decision was made. She grabbed her coat from the hall stand and bolted.

Katy wasn't stupid, but given the circumstances, she found it difficult to think clearly. One thing she did know, however, was that now she'd made her choice, she had to get as far away from here as she possibly could. Her first port of call was the super-market where she withdrew two hundred pounds from the 'hole in the wall'. From there she made her way to the station.

"Can I help you, Madam? Do you want to buy a ticket?" the clerk asked.

Katy fumbled with her purse. She hadn't a clue where to go.

Finally, she said, "Scotland, I want to travel to Scotland." She wouldn't just move town she'd move country. Gordon would never find her there.

"Scotland is a big place," the clerk said. "Did you have a particular town in mind, or should I just guess," he added sarcastically.

Overwhelmed by the question she began to cry. The clerk relented.

"It's getting rather late in the day, but you're still in time to catch a train going to Glasgow. Would that suit you?"

The truth was she had no idea whether it suited her or not, but, nevertheless, within ten minutes she was sitting on a train headed north. She was aware of other passengers staring at her and little wonder, her face was tear-stained, her hair dishevelled, and all her worldly goods were stuffed into a duvet cover which was decorated with overblown pink roses. She must look a very strange sight. Katy opened her handbag, removed a tissue, her hairbrush, and her make-up bag, intending to tidy herself up when she spotted her house keys at the bottom of the bag. The realisation that she'd never be returning to her home, to the rooms she'd lovingly decorated, the furniture she'd saved up to buy, and all her precious ornaments and knick-knacks made her weep again.

"Are you alright? Are you feeling ill?" a man's voice cut through her misery, and she looked up to see a tall, handsome, athletic-looking man.

He slid into the seat at the opposite side of the table. "This really is my seat. See fourteen B, it's on my ticket. Honest, I'm not trying to come onto you." He held out his ticket for her to see. "I'm going all the way to Glasgow Central," he continued.

She held her hand in front of her mouth, holding back a sob and stared silently at the man.

"I'm getting a coffee from the buffet car. Do you want one?

By the way, my name's John." He offered her his hand to shake, and she automatically accepted.

"Katy, my name's Katy, and I've just left my husband."

"Is that who gave you the shiner?" he asked, nodding towards her rapidly blackening eye.

Her hand immediately touched her face and fresh tears filled her eyes once again.

"Sit tight and I'll be back in a minute with the coffees. Don't upset yourself. The worst is over. You're safe here."

As John disappeared down the carriageway Katy sat with her head in her hands and her elbows resting on the table in front of her. What have I done, she thought to herself, what on earth have I done?

A wave of nausea swept over her, and she realised she hadn't eaten for several hours. Her morning sickness, for some reason, seemed to appear at any time of the day, especially when she was hungry, so she was grateful when John reappeared carrying not only the coffees but sandwich packs and chocolate biscuits as well.

"Thank you, you're very kind," she said staring into his soft green eyes.

"You look like you could do with a break," he replied. "I know what it's like to be hurt and alone," he added. Then he looked down and cleared his throat as if he was embarrassed.

"Did someone special leave you?" she asked.

"In a manner of speaking," John replied. "My wife died last year. I woke up one morning and she was dead beside me. The doctors said it was an undetected heart condition. I still can't believe she's gone. Carol and I were childhood sweethearts. We went to primary school together. I loved her all my life."

"I'm so sorry," Katy replied. She didn't know what else to say.

There was an awkward silence for a minute or two then John said, "Help yourself to a sandwich I wasn't sure what you'd fancy so you have a choice of roast beef or chicken. I hope you're not a vegetarian or I'm afraid I've got it completely wrong."

As she ate, the nausea passed, and Katy found herself telling John her life history. Word after word, sentence after sentence poured out of her and as she spoke, she felt unburdened. She realised that her entire life had been spent running away from one thing after another. Her first flight had been to university to escape the family home and her cold, controlling father. Then when he died, she returned home to support her mother. She couldn't stand living within the confines of the house. She'd forgotten about her mother's obsessive compulsion to clean and tidy at all times of the day and night. It drove her mad. She'd had four years of making her own decisions at university. She liked being able to leave her clothes in a heap if she chose, but living at home made her feel stifled, claustrophobic. Then Gordon came along and offered her a way out. She thought he loved her. He called her his uptown girl, and she was. She came from a middle-class background whereas his family were working class. Katy had run to him with open arms. Now she was running again.

"So let me get this straight," John said. "You have a degree, had a good job with prospects, and you were paying all the bills. Gordon has little education, got fired from a dead-end job for stealing, he hit you, and you feel guilty about leaving him. Why? You have nothing to feel guilty about."

"He was frustrated being out of work. My successes made him feel inadequate. I shouldn't have moaned about his drinking. I knew he'd get upset."

"Stop making excuses for him, woman," John said. "Can't you see his kind of love is destructive? He was a ticking bomb. Anything could have set him off. It's lucky you found the strength to run."

"I don't know what to do," Katy said voicing her fears aloud. "I've walked out on my job, walked out on my home, and I'm three months pregnant," she added almost in a whisper. "I have seven hundred pounds in my bank account and about a hundred and sixty in cash and I'm heading towards a strange city where I don't know a soul. I don't even know what I'll do when this train arrives in Glasgow."

CHAPTER TWO

When John Houston jumped on the train at the last minute before it was due to leave, he had no idea that within a short while he'd be pouring his heart out to a complete stranger. Until now, he'd been unable to discuss Carol's death with anyone, not even his own mother. His mum, Betty, had loved her and said she was the daughter she'd never had. Everybody loved her, but no one more than John.

From the first day he'd met her he'd adored her. They were five years old, and their mums had just left them at the local primary school. Carol was tough. The youngest of four children, she had three older brothers. She could play football better than any of the boys, and she was clever, already reading basic books by the time she came to school. She wasn't the prettiest girl in class, Emily Andrews held that title, but she had a cute face with small, even features and her hair was the colour of spun gold.

John and Carol lived only one street away from each other and they became inseparable friends. It was almost inevitable their friendship would turn to love as neither could imagine ever being apart. Both families were delighted when they wed, and everyone got on so well together it was hard to know where one family ended and the other began.

Both John and Carol loved children and hoped to have a large family, but they sensibly agreed to wait until they felt emotionally ready and financially secure. John finished his degree then began his academic life lecturing at the university in social sciences. He wrote textbooks and was paid handsomely to deliver lectures all over the country. Carol trained as a baker then developed her own company supplying cup cakes to shops just at the time they became popular. So, all in all, they were quite comfortably off when they planned for a family and Carol stopped taking the pill. Three months later she was dead.

"Can you help me please? I'm not sure where to go when we get off the train," Katy's voice cut through his thoughts. "I'll have to book into a hotel for tonight at least. Can you recommend something close to the station that won't turn me away when they see my stylish luggage," she joked nodding at the duvet cover.

John stared at the pretty blonde woman facing him and thought of his large sandstone house. It had four bedrooms. He and Carol had bought it with the intention of filling it with children. Now he rattled around in it like a marble in a jar. Katy seemed so vulnerable, slender, and petite that her large blue eyes looked haunted. For a moment he considered inviting her to stay, but he knew it wouldn't be appropriate on so many levels.

"When we leave the station, I'm catching a taxi home. I'll drop you at the Premier Inn on my way. It'll be quite basic but it's clean and cheap and you can walk into town from there simply by crossing the bridge over the River Clyde."

"Cheap sounds good," she replied. "It's been a traumatic day, but I'm sure I'll feel better able to sort myself out after a night's sleep. I suppose I'll have to get myself to a job centre and register as unemployed and I'll have to find somewhere to live. My money will soon run out if I remain in a hotel."

John stared at Katy for a couple of moments then he said, "I might be able to help you. My brother-in-law is a property developer, and I know he's almost completed the renovation of a small flat on the south side of the city which he plans to rent out. When I say small, I mean tiny. Just a studio flat really, but housing benefit would cover the rent until you found work and it would be cheap enough for you to afford after you secure employment. Why don't you take my card," he said, fishing one out of his wallet and handing it to her. "Call me tomorrow after four. I'll have finished lecturing by then and I'll be able to tell you what I've found out."

"You're so kind," Katy said, and fresh tears filled her eyes. "You know nothing about me and yet here you are offering me support."

John was embarrassed. He didn't know what to say so instead he took his blackberry from his pocket, cleared his throat, and looked up the number for the Premier Inn.

"It'll be better if we make your booking now," he explained. "Then you'll just have to check in. Besides, I might manage to get you a discounted rate by using my university connection. We give them lots of business so I'll see what I can do."

It was then Katy realised that she hadn't lifted her mobile when she'd run. She could visualise it clearly, lying on the kitchen table. However, she reasoned, it was only a pay as you go phone and easily replaceable and at least Gordon wouldn't be able to contact her. She could soon buy a new phone and have a fresh start.

By the time the train entered Glasgow Central station Katy Bradley had a reservation at the hotel for two nights. When asking her name to make the booking and after a discussion about it, John remarked that it was lucky she hadn't adopted Gordon's surname when they'd married.

"At least you won't have the added complication of changing your bank details and passport now that you and Gordon have separated," he said.

Katy hadn't got as far as thinking about the practicalities of her situation she was simply relieved to know that she'd have a roof over her head for the night. When the train finally rolled to a halt, she was overwhelmed by exhaustion. Her limbs felt leaden, and she had a dull ache in her back. If John hadn't taken her arm and helped her to her feet, she doubted she could have managed to get off the train. He lifted her belongings for her and, with his own rucksack looped over his shoulder, led her towards the taxi stance. It was a foul night, dark, cold, and raining.

"Welcome to Glasgow," he said wryly. "Are you going to be okay?" he enquired. "You're as white as a sheet."

"I'm just exhausted," she replied. "It's been a very upsetting day. I'll be all right once I get a cup of tea and a warm bath. I can't wait to climb into bed. I feel as if I could sleep for a week."

There was a taxi waiting at the stand and the journey to the hotel took less than ten minutes. John asked the driver to wait while he helped her inside. The receptionist gave them a curious look when he eyed her belongings, but he said nothing. He'd seen stranger things in his job, much stranger. Once John knew she was booked in, he took his leave of her, but before exiting he turned.

"Remember to call after four," he said. "You've still got my card, haven't you? By four o'clock, with a bit of luck, I'll have some information for you."

"Thank you, John, you've been very kind. I'll call you tomorrow. I do have your card," she said taking it from her coat pocket and holding it aloft.

Within a few minutes Katy was in the lift ascending to her hotel room and John was back in the taxi heading for his home. By the time she reached the room the effort of dragging her belongings from the lift had been almost too much for her. She managed to pull the duvet cover over the threshold and close the door then she flopped down onto the bed completely spent. All thoughts of having a warm bath and a cup of tea were abandoned. Instead, she stripped down to her underwear and slid between the sheets. Her bones were aching. She still had the dull ache in her back and a thumping headache as well. I'll just have a bit of a rest, she thought then I'll sort myself out. Within a couple of minutes, she was sound asleep.

All the way home in the cab John worried about Katy. Had he done the wrong thing in leaving her at the hotel, he wondered. She looked awful. What if she was ill and became worse through the night? She was on her own with no one to check on her. She might be getting worse, and he'd left her to fend for herself. What if she died?

"Oh, for God's sake, stop being an idiot," he muttered to himself. "She's a stranger I met on a train, and she probably won't even call me."

Within twenty minutes he was home, back to his big empty house. John poured himself a large scotch, switched on the television to help him relax and pushed all thoughts of Katy Bradley from his mind.

CHAPTER THREE

Katy was woken at dawn by the loud chirping of birds in the trees outside her window. Then almost immediately her body was wracked with pain. Her lower back felt as if it was gripped in a vice and she was doubled up with agonising stomach cramps. The bed felt damp, and she wondered if she'd wet herself in her sleep. It took her a few moments to process what was happening then, as another agonising spasm of pain gripped her belly, she realised. It's the baby, I'm losing the baby, she thought. She was scared, she had to get help. She reached for the telephone beside the bed and managed to press zero for reception. When the receptionist answered, with her knees bent up to her chest and the phone pressed into the pillow, Katy gasped, "Help me," before passing out.

"It's all right, Pet, I'm going to look after you. Don't be scared, I'm a paramedic. I'm just going to attach this drip to give you fluids and I'm going to put this monitor on your finger. Can you tell me your name?"

"Katy, I'm Katy Bradley," she replied trying to focus through the blur of pain.

"Good girl, Katy. Now can you tell me if you've taken anything? Any tablets or drugs?"

"I think I'm losing my baby. I'm three months pregnant," she sobbed as another crushing spasm gripped her.

She heard the paramedic say to her colleague, "Spontaneous abortion, I think. We'd better take her to the Southern General."

"I haven't done anything," Katy cried. "I'd never hurt my baby. I'd never have an abortion."

"Yes, Pet, we know. We think you're having a miscarriage. I'm sorry, Pet, but the sooner we get you to the hospital the sooner we'll know what's happening. Try to stay calm."

Katy sobbed quietly as the paramedics wrapped her in a blanket, strapped her to a chair and carried her to the waiting ambulance. The fifteen minutes it took them to reach the hospital was a journey filled with pain and despair. Within a few minutes of arriving, she was examined then whisked off to theatre. When she woke, she was groggy, but she knew she was no longer pregnant. She wept for her lost child, and she grieved for her lost marriage and the life she should have had.

The doctors wanted to keep her in hospital for a couple of days as her blood pressure was fluctuating. The hotel was very efficient and later that day the staff arranged for her belongings to be delivered to the ward. When she felt able, Katy searched for John's card so she could call him and explain what had happened, but somehow it had been mislaid, it wasn't amongst her things. She felt terrible. After being so kind to her he would now think she'd never intended to call, but at this point in time, there was nothing she could do.

...

John woke bright and early and drove to the university. He parked in his allocated space and made his way to his office. He didn't have to deliver his lecture until eleven o'clock, so he decided to phone his brother-in-law Peter to ask about the studio apartment. He wanted to have all the information about it before Katy called. He decided not to tell Peter too much about her or the circumstances of their meeting. He didn't want him to get the wrong idea and read something into it that wasn't there.

Before he had the opportunity to make his call the telephone rang.

"Hello," he answered, "John Houston. Who's calling, please?"

"Hi John, Patrick Cosgrove here from the University of Manchester, how are you doing mate? I'm just calling to let you know we've had the funding approved for your proposal. They met up and agreed just after you left. So, it looks like you'll be coming down here for three months beginning next week. It's all been cleared with both of our universities."

"That's fantastic news, have you arranged a room in the halls of residence for me?"

"Not on your Nelly. You'll stay with me. Like you, I'm on my own and I've got a large house. If you don't mind, we can be company for each other."

"Thanks Patrick, I could do with some company. I spend far too much time on my own. It's really good of you to offer. I haven't stayed in halls for years, but from what I remember, they're very cramped and full of spotty teenagers."

"That's settled then," Patrick replied. "I'll call you at home later and we can make our arrangements. I'm looking forward to working with you, mate."

After he came off the phone John punched the air with delight, "Yes," he said triumphantly. The sole purpose for his recent trip south was to answer some final questions regarding funding and now it had been approved. He was excited. This would allow him to complete his research. It was the break he needed to help him move on with his life. He felt a bit sorry that he wouldn't be around to help Katy because he liked the girl, in a strange way her fragility made him feel strong. But with a bit of luck Peter would soon have a new tenant and she'd get a quality roof over her head and a caring landlord. Besides, he could keep in touch by phone if he chose.

John dialled his brother-in-law's number, and the call was answered on the third ring. After some brief banter he wrote down the information about the flat and told him of his impending trip.

"It'll do you good to get a break," Peter said. "We all know how hard it's been for you since Carol died. We all miss her terribly. Don't worry about your house I'll look after things for you. I'll even cut the grass."

"Thanks, Peter, I'll call you later with the details of the prospective tenant if she gets in touch."

They talked for a few minutes more before John ended the call to prepare for his lecture. All through the day he felt a buzz of excitement every time he thought about his research grant. In another couple of days his work here would stop for the summer, and he'd be free to go. When the word went round, his colleagues came to congratulate him and to wish him well. Then, apart from one repeat lecture he was giving due to public demand, his day was his own.

With all the comings and goings John didn't notice that the day was almost over until he saw the cleaners in the hallway. When he glanced at his phone, which was still switched to silent for his lecture, he realised it was after five and Katy hadn't called. He checked his messages, but she definitely hadn't been in touch. He was disappointed. Stupidly disappointed, after all, she was a complete stranger to him. He knew nothing about her apart from what she'd told him and that might be a load of bollocks. He felt like an idiot now for calling Peter about the apartment. But, he reasoned, life was never as simple as it seemed. At least he now had plans for the summer and, with any luck, by the autumn he and Patrick would have a paper ready with some cutting-edge theories to report.

...

Katy lay in her hospital bed and contemplated her loss. She felt very depressed. The next day a hospital social worker paid her a visit and Katy poured her heart out to her.

"Oh dear, what an awful time you've had," the woman said sympathetically. "I can help you with the practical things, but I'll arrange a counsellor if you'd like to talk about the way you feel. Don't worry the system is in place to help people in your situation. You won't have to cope on your own."

Although the social worker was very kind and said all the right things, she had never felt so alone. She wished she still had John's card. The kind stranger was strong and for a short while he'd taken care of her. She felt vulnerable and weak and, more than anything, she yearned for him to be beside her now.

CHAPTER FOUR

$\mathcal{E}$ventually, after three days, Katy's blood pressure returned to normal, and she was discharged from the hospital. She was met in a taxi by Tricia, her allocated social worker, who took her to a women's refuge on the south side of the city. It was far from ideal, very basic accommodation with shared facilities, but beggars can't be choosers. She qualified for a place because she was fleeing from domestic violence. The real downside to her situation was that all the other women who resided there were accompanied by children. It made her all the more bereft for no longer being pregnant.

The next few days passed in a blur as she visited the job centre, housing benefit office, and social work department. She also registered with a doctor for her on-going care. Her endeavours left her completely exhausted, so it was no surprise when she developed a virus and was forced to spend a couple of days in bed.

"I've brought you some chicken soup, Hen," Marie, one of her fellow guests said as she opened the door and looked in. "It's just out of a packet, 'Knorr', I think. I cannae cook myself, but it'll warm you through and make you feel better. My maw used to swear by it."

Katy pushed herself into a sitting position and gratefully took the soup mug from Marie, "Thank you, you're very kind," she replied and suddenly found herself blubbering.

"Dinnae worry about greetin' Hen. It's just your hormones 'cause you lost your bairn. We've all suffered loss in this place, and we all feel for you. When you're up to it, come and join us in the lounge, and I'll introduce you to some of the other girls. We're a mixed bunch so dinnae worry about being English. We'll forgive you," she added, laughing.

Katy thanked Marie and sipped the hot soup. It was probably more psychological than medicinal, but soon she felt better and climbed out of bed. Quickly she dressed, pulled a comb through her hair, and washed her face. Then she rooted around in her belongings until she found the packet of biscuits she'd bought in case she wanted a sweet snack and, with it clutched in her hand, made her way to the lounge.

The room was large and sparsely furnished with mismatched chairs. There was an acrid, singed smell coming from the electric bar heaters the women were huddled around. The air smelled fuggy, and the room felt cold and rather damp despite the sun shining through the windows. Marie stood when she saw Katy.

"In you come, Hen. Have this seat beside Kelly and I'll make us some tea. It'll have to be black because the milk's finished. Do you take sugar?"

Katy handed over the biscuits she'd brought. "One spoon, please," she answered, and she took the seat she'd been offered.

Before going off to the kitchen to put the kettle on, Marie quickly introduced the other two girls who were sitting in the room.

"She's called Nadia," Marie said nodding towards an Asian

girl wearing a green sari. "And this is Kelly," she said placing her hand on the shoulder of a heavily pregnant girl.

Kelly was very skinny apart from her enormous bump. She looked about twelve. She was dressed in a short shift and had bare legs. Her hair was thin and limp, and her skin pasty and pockmarked.

"This is my third and it's a boy this time," Kelly said patting her bump. "It makes no difference though my man still doesn't want it. My two girls are with my mum," she explained.

"And will you stay with your mum after the baby's born?" Katy asked.

"Not a chance. We can't stand each other. I suppose I'll give her the baby then I'll go back to my man. He's only violent when I'm pregnant because he doesn't want kids. It's always been my fault 'cause if we've had a drink, I sometimes forget to take the pill. I'm having my tubes tied after this one so every-thing will be okay, and it won't happen again. I asked them to do it the last time after I had my Chelsea, but they said I was too young."

"You look very young now," Katy said unable to stop herself.

"I'm not young," Kelly replied laughing. "I'm nearly nine-teen. I was fifteen when I had my first."

Katy looked down, trying not to show the shock she felt. At that moment Marie came back in with the teas.

"Pull that table over Nadia," she said gesticulating to the girl. "Nadia's here because her husband's family think she's hurt their honour. Her daughter is in school round the corner, but her boys are with their dad in Dundee. She's left her man because he battered her and nearly killed her. Her own family won't take her back. They'd rather see the lassie dead than leave her man. It's no use trying to talk to her. She's nearly deaf from the battering and she dinnae speak much English. She's from India or Pakistan. One of thay foreign places, so if you want to talk to her, you'll have to use your hands to explain."

"Just like her husband did," Kelly said wryly. "I know you lost your baby and I'm sorry if my pregnancy is in your face," she said, turning to Katy. "If you want to talk about it that's fine, if not, that's fine too."

"There's not much to tell," Katy began. "I got pregnant. My husband lost his job. He spent all his time in the pub and a few days ago he got angry and hit me, so I ran away."

"Did he punch your belly?" Kelly asked. "Is that why you lost the baby?"

"No, nothing like that, he just slapped my face and gave me a black eye."

Kelly stared at her incredulously. "And you left him because of one slap. It might have been a one-off. I've been in the hospital twice. My man's broken my jaw, my wrist, some ribs and once he dislocated my shoulder."

"And you keep going back for more," Marie said. "Katy here's got the right idea. Get out before it gets worse. I met a girl called Jessie once and she kept going back even after her man had been in the jail. She's dead now and her man's battering some other poor cow."

Katy drank her tea, it tasted stewed. Then she suggested they all go out for a walk to get some air.

"We dinnae go out and walk about unless we absolutely have to," Marie explained. "We don't want to risk being seen or someone might tell our men where we are. It's all right for you because your man lives in England. He won't think to look for you here."

"Not for a while anyway," Kelly added.

"Aye, not for a while," Marie agreed, "But they find you eventually if they want to."

At that moment Tricia popped her head round the door.

"I've got some papers for you to sign," she said to Katy who immediately stood up, said goodbye to the girls and, grateful for the social worker's interruption, quickly exited the room.

When they were seated in her room Katy said, "I have to get out of this place. I'm grateful for the roof over my head, but I hate it here. What are my options?"

Tricia explained that within a few weeks the council would offer her some kind of accommodation, but it would probably not be in an area she'd like.

"Your neighbours might be junkies or alcoholics. You're almost at the bottom of the pile for a flat because you're young, single, and without kids. You're only here because you've miscarried and are fleeing from violence. There is the private sector if you can put together a deposit, but many landlords won't take people on benefits, so the most important thing is to find a job. Do you think it's worth contacting your previous employer to explain why you left? Do you think they might give you a reference?"

"It's possible," Katy replied. "At the very least they deserve an apology. I worked for them for three years. I'll try calling, and I'll see if I can speak to Mr. Reynolds. He was my manager. I'll let you know how I get on."

Katy and Tricia chatted some more then they left the building together. Katy wanted to look round the city centre to properly get her bearings. Tricia said she was calling for a taxi and offered to drop her in town on the way to her next call. It was clear from their conversation both women felt, that with a bit of effort, Katy could improve her position.

CHAPTER FIVE

When Tricia's taxi dropped Katy off outside the St. Enoch shopping centre, in the heart of the city, the first thing she did was locate a mobile phone shop and buy a pay-as-you-go phone. She paid for twenty pounds worth of calls to be added, then asked the young man who served her for directions to the nearest employment agency. After consulting his computer, he wrote down the addresses of three establishments. All were close to the shop and just a couple of minutes walk from each other.

I've got to be positive and start as I mean to go on, she thought. Surely with her qualifications and experience someone would want to employ her, especially if she telephoned Mr. Reynolds and he was prepared to give her a reference. One thing she knew for sure was that she couldn't stay in the refuge. Although the other women were kind, she had nothing in common with any of them and whilst it was clean, warm, and safe, she was used to better, much better.

The first two agencies Katy called on had her complete application forms and said they'd be in touch if something turned up. She felt her spirits sink as the realisation of her position became clear. All her experience was with large insurance companies and many of these companies were laying people off rather than hiring. It was with a heavy heart that she entered the third agency. Once again, she filled out the registration form. This time, however, she was surprised to be invited into an interview room instead of being politely shown to the door. Soon she was pouring her heart out to a kind young man with an easy smile and startling blue eyes.

"I like your honesty," the agent, whose name was Gregor, said. "Do you think your previous employer will give you a reference? The job I have in mind isn't the same calibre as you're used to, but you could do the work with your eyes closed. It's in a small brokerage on the south side of town. They need someone familiar with the products they handle and who can start within two weeks."

"I'll phone my previous boss. I'm sure when he knows the circumstances of my leaving, he'll give me a reference. I was very reliable, and I didn't miss a single day's work in three years. Please just give me a few minutes to call him. I really need this job," Katy pleaded.

"Look, I'm sympathetic of your situation. My sister was married to a violent man," Gregor replied. "Take your time. I'm going nowhere for the next hour at least."

"Thank you, thank you so much," she said. "You're very kind."

"Everyone needs a break," he replied, and he showed her back to the outer office so she could make her call.

Katy took some time to prepare in her mind what she was going to say, but when she dialled the number and the phone was answered by Betty, the receptionist, she found herself blurting out her story and bursting into tears.

"Oh, you poor, poor lass," Betty said. "I'm so sorry you and Gordon have split up. You always seemed such a together couple."

Katy hadn't mentioned precisely why they'd separated or that she'd been pregnant and lost the baby. She found that piece of information tough to get her head around and thought it would be better if she kept it to herself. Within a couple of minutes, she was put through to Mr. Reynolds and she tearfully related her story once again.

"You left us completely in the lurch," he said. "A simple telephone call would have been nice. However, I do understand how upset you must be and while you were here you were a model employee, so yes, I would be prepared to give you a reference. Please furnish Betty with a contact telephone number and a correspondence address and we'll send on any documentation you're due. Your final pay will be paid into your bank as usual."

Katy couldn't stop grinning. Her heart was thumping in her chest. She thanked Mr. Reynolds profusely then after hanging up the phone, returned to Gregor's office.

"Just because I put you forward for the job, doesn't mean you'll get it," he warned. "They'll probably interview at least four people for the post, but I can tell you that I think on paper at least, you'll be the best candidate. I'll call you and let you know once an interview is set up. The rest will be up to you."

Katy practically skipped out of the office, she was so happy to be given a chance, but after a few minutes she suddenly felt exhausted. She was still recovering from the miscarriage and felt dragged down by the virus she was fighting off. The hustle and bustle of the busy town centre was tiring and the very thought of trying to locate the correct bus to take her back to the refuge was overwhelming. Throwing caution to the wind, she decided to spoil herself by hailing a taxi, reasoning that her health and well-being were more important than saving the money it would cost.

...

GORDON WAITED a week after Katy walked out before trying to find her. He thought she'd run to her mum's house and was surprised and angry when he discovered she wasn't there. He'd run out of food and drinking money and the house was a mess. Eventually, he phoned his sister Annie to try to borrow money. He was drunk as usual and when he whined about Katy walking out over one little slap, she showed him no sympathy.

"Good on her. Serves you right," Annie said. "You don't deserve her. You're just like Dad. I hope she makes a fresh start and never comes back."

"Just phone me if you hear from her," Gordon replied angrily. "You're meant to support me," he added. "I'm your family."

"More's the pity," Annie replied. "I hope she does phone me so I can congratulate her for seeing sense. Please don't call here again. I'll not be giving you any money to support your drinking habit, and I won't tell you if she gets in touch. Why don't you get help to dry out and stop feeling sorry for yourself?"

"Well thanks for nothing, Sis. I'll find her myself and when I do, she'll be sorry," he threatened before ending the call and hurling the phone across the room. "Women are all bitches," he said aloud, "Bloody, ball-breaking bitches."

...

AS KATY CLIMBED out of the taxi at the refuge the front door was thrown open and a boy aged about ten was attempting to flee down the stairs into the street. He'd made it almost to the bottom when he was unceremoniously grabbed by Marie. Her face looked thunderous.

"What have I told you about hitting girls?" she screamed. "Do you want to end up like your dad?"

The boy began to protest. "But, Mum, she hit me first. She was starting with me when I was trying to do my project for school."

"Then you come and tell me about it. You never, ever hit your sister or any girl for that matter. Do you understand?"

The boy meekly nodded his agreement, but Katy could see by his expression that he felt he was being treated unfairly.

"Now go inside and finish your work. If your sister comes near you again, tell her I'm coming in to deal with her and I said they'll be no 'Coronation Street' tonight."

The boy perked up. "I'll tell her, Mum," he said, smiling.

"Kids, who'd have 'em?" Marie said, turning to Katy, then immediately, "Oh, I'm so sorry, Hen. You must think I'm heartless saying that after your loss. I dinnae mean to hurt you. Sometimes I open my mouth and put both feet in."

"It's okay, Marie," Katy replied. "I'm all right."

"Look at you, coming home in a taxi, eh," Marie said, changing the subject, "Your social worker must be made of money."

Katy wasn't sure about the politics of the refuge, so she said nothing about paying for the cab herself. As much as she hated being there, she didn't want to alienate herself from the rest of the women.

"I hope you'll excuse me, Marie," she said. "I'm rather tired. I guess it'll take a while for me to get my strength back. I'm going to my room to lie down and get a little rest."

"Aye, you do that, Hen," Marie replied. "The lounge is full of weans at the moment. They're doing ma heed in, and I'm used to the noise they make. Do you want me to knock on your door when 'Corrie' starts?"

Katy could think of nothing worse than being stuck in front

of the television with a group of battered women exchanging their tales of woe while surrounded by their noisy children.

"No thanks," she replied. "I think at the moment I need rest more than anything. I'm so tired I might even sleep through the night."

"Okay, Hen, dinnae you worry, I can tell you about it tomorrow. Then you'll know what's happened before Friday's episode."

As she wearily climbed the stairs to her room the noise from the lounge reached a crescendo. There were thuds and crashes, adults yelling, children screaming, and the television was blasting out some repetitive dance number. Katy once again found herself weeping. She didn't know how long she could stand living in this awful place, but where else could she go? Until Tricia found her a place of her own, she was trapped here and even if she was offered something, it might be worse. At least here she was safe.

CHAPTER SIX

John Houston hadn't realised just how isolated he'd become until he moved south of the border to work with Patrick. He was used to coming home and spending his evenings poring over his work with his head in a book or dozing in front of the telly. He hadn't had the strength or the inclination to do much else. Now Patrick was showing him a calendar on the kitchen wall listing pub quizzes, invites to parties, a monthly dinner club, dart's nights, bowling nights and the list went on and on.

"There's quite a few of us singles living here," Patrick explained. "I rather enjoy my own company, but nobody wants to be lonely. There is a difference you see, and the difference is having a choice."

Patrick's home was a modern, four bedrooms, two bath-rooms, detached, in a very upmarket area. It was nothing like John's traditional red-sandstone terraced house, but comfortable and spacious, nevertheless. For the first time in a long time John felt as if he was back in the world. For months he'd shut himself away, cut himself off so he wouldn't have to face people. He didn't want to share his grief with anyone, and he definitely didn't want to talk about his loss.

At first, he felt shy about joining in, particularly if there were women in the group, but after a couple of weeks he was back to his old self, joking and participating in banter with the rest of the guys. Now that he was feeling better about his life in general, from time to time he thought about the sad, fragile girl he'd met on the train and wondered what had become of her. He was sorry she hadn't got in touch, but he knew only too well about keeping your distance from other people as a way of protecting yourself.

The two men began their work the week after John arrived and it immediately became clear that it was a marriage made in heaven.

"If we'd known how well we'd get on, both socially and academically, we could have been collaborating on projects long before this," Patrick said.

"I'm really pleased the funding committee came through with the money," John agreed. "It's absolutely true what they say, there is strength in numbers. The committee obviously felt two heads were better than one. Perhaps we should apply for a European grant on the strength of what we produce this time. Maybe next year you could visit me in Glasgow, though I can't guarantee the same social life."

"Perhaps," Patrick pondered. "Or we could say we want to do research somewhere else like the Munich Beer Festival or the Cannes Film Festival or how about the Valencia Grand Prix. As long as we stick to Europe they might just say yes."

John chuckled, "You believe in pushing your luck, don't you mate."

"If you don't ask, you don't get," Patrick replied. "And on that subject, Penny Miller has recently divorced her deadbeat husband. Why don't we invite her and Jenny Archer out for dinner? After all, they're two single girls, we're two single guys.

For the price of some pub grub and a bottle of wine we might just get lucky."

"You're incorrigible," John replied. "You know that don't you?"

He didn't want to let his friend down by refusing, but he felt rather uncomfortable about going on what might be perceived as a date, even if it was just dinner at the local pub.

KATY WAS EXCITED when she received the call about her interview, and she quickly ran downstairs to tell Marie.

"I have a smart suit to wear, but I left my black court shoes behind when I ran and my hair's a total mess," she said.

"I'll cut your hair," Pat, one of the other girls, offered. "Sorry for listening in, but everyone in this place craves good news. I'm a trained hairdresser so don't worry, I won't butcher it. If I cut it in long layers, it will look fuller."

"You can try on my black funeral shoes," another girl, called Lisa, said. "I've only worn them twice and your feet look about the same size as mine. I take a size five and a half."

Katy got a lump in her throat. How kind these women were. They had virtually nothing except breaks and bruises and yet here they were offering the little they did have to a virtual stranger. How unfair she'd been by judging them as if she was superior. She felt ashamed.

"Your handbag looks a bit tatty," Kelly said. Katy's eyes were downcast. "Sorry, I didn't mean to be rude. You can borrow my 'Prada'. It's not the real thing of course, but it's plain and black and it'll go with Lisa's shoes."

Katy found herself weeping.

"Oh, stop crying, you silly cow," Marie scolded. "Do you think we don't know what you're going through? You've got a real chance of getting your life back, a chance to escape from this dump. Every single one of us would jump through hoops for that opportunity. Right, you lot," she said to the group, "Get your stuff and we'll meet in the kitchen. We'll make a start on that bird's nest Katy calls a hairstyle." She turned to Katy and said, "You'd better get the damned job because after we sort you out, you'll owe us a drink and we won't let you forget it in a hurry."

For the next two hours her hair was trimmed and tweaked, Pat even gave her highlights. There was a real party atmosphere in the kitchen, more so after Katy gave Lisa money to run to the off-licence for a litre of white wine. By the time she'd been made up and tried on her outfit, with the borrowed shoes and hand-bag, she felt like a million dollars. With mugs of wine in their hands the women stepped back from her to admire their work.

"Oh, Hen, you look gorgeous. I could fancy you myself," Marie said, mouthing a kiss.

"Our experience with men is enough to turn anyone gay," Lisa added, and they all hooted with laughter.

"I havnae laughed this much for ages, Hen," Marie said. "You're a breath of fresh air. What time's your interview tomorrow?"

"Ten o'clock at a place called Queenspark. Is that far from here? I haven't a clue where I'm going."

"What's the address?" Pat asked. "I know that area, I grew up there."

"Victoria Road, the company's called McLay and Bell."

"Right, that's easy peasy. Victoria Road is the main road and it's only one stop on the train. If Marie takes my Brian to school for me, I'll come with you and show you how to get there."

"Aye, nae problem, Pat, we cannae have the lassie getting lost. Not when we've put in such a lot of work to make her look good."

"Thank you all so much. You're amazing. I'll never forget what you've done for me," Katy said.

"Oh yes you will," Lisa said. "You'll get a job, and you'll get a flat and, if you're smart, you'll run away from here as fast as you can and never look back. Every one of us would do the same. We support and help each other while we're here, but this isn't a normal life. We've been thrown together, and we do the best we can, but really, we're all strangers."

"Aye, she's right, Hen. Once we're free from this place, we won't want to think about it ever again," Marie said, and the others nodded in agreement.

On that rather sombre note the women left the kitchen and went their separate ways.

"Meet me at the front door at nine o'clock tomorrow," Pat called as she headed up the stairs to her room. "That will give you plenty of time to find the place and we'll avoid the rush hour."

Katy felt a shudder of anticipation run down her spine. Maybe tomorrow would herald a new beginning, the start of a better life.

CHAPTER SEVEN

Katy took a last glance in the mirror before going downstairs to meet Pat. Finally, a familiar face stared back at her. She didn't know if it was her no-nonsense suit or the light make-up she'd applied, but she looked every bit like a young professional. By contrast Pat wore a short, red skirt topped by a thin, grey sweater, her bomber-style jacket was synthetic to mimic leather, her legs were bare, and she sported plastic flip-flops on her feet. They looked an unlikely pair.

"Would you look at you," Pat said approvingly. "I feel as if I'm going out with Victoria Beckham or the Queen. Don't you scrub up well? It's the hair that makes the difference, of course."

"Of course," Katy agreed, and they both laughed.

It took them very little time to reach their destination. They easily located the premises of McLay and Bell then spent the next twenty minutes trawling the many charity shops for bargains. Katy treated Pat to a stylish raincoat that cost five pounds and she reacted as if she'd been bought diamonds. Katy realised then that her companion had never owned much and had few aspirations. Trained as a hairdresser she'd been the most qualified of any of her family. The only shining light in her life was her son, Brian, whom she adored.

Katy glanced at her watch. "Well," she said, "It's time for me to go. Wish me luck."

"Do you want me to come with you? I could sit in the front office and wait if you'd like. We could tell them I'm your sister."

Katy couldn't think of anything worse or a more unlikely lie.

"Thanks for offering, but I'm a big girl and I've got to do this myself."

She gave Pat the three pounds fifty pence of change she had in her purse so the girl could get a coffee in the nearby cafe. Pat said she'd wait there until Katy returned. Then, shaking slightly with nerves, she made her way to the brokerage and inhaling deeply, entered through the shop front door.

"I'm, ah, here for an interview," she stammered to the smiling woman seated at a desk near the counter.

"Katy Bradley?" the woman asked then said. "Hi, I'm Sandra. David Bell will be with you shortly. He's just finishing a telephone call now."

The office was modern and bright, and a vase of fresh flowers stood on the counter. Within a couple of minutes, she was shown through to Mr. Bell's room which was situated at the back of the building, and was offered a cup of coffee. It was all very relaxed. David Bell, a man in his forties, was short of stature, slightly plump with a receding hairline and a friendly smile. After a formal introduction he went on to explain the office hierarchy.

"There is no 'McLay', there hasn't been for years. He was a contemporary of my father's. I am the broker and Martin Campbell is my assistant, he's out on a call at the moment. We are all on first name terms here. It's a small office and I can't be doing with formalities. You met Sandra. She manages the office, and the other girl is Pamela. Deborah, who you'll be replacing, is on maternity leave, but it's unlikely she'll return after the birth. I've seen your CV that the agency sent, I'm satisfied you understand what's required and you're more than qualified for the post. We're inundated with work at the moment, so I've decided not to waste anybody's time by carrying out multiple interviews. If you think you'd like to work here, the job's yours. Is there anything you'd like to ask me?"

Katy was stunned. She didn't know what to say. "When would you like me to start?" she finally managed.

David glanced at the calendar on his desk, "A week on Monday is the first of the month, so if you could start then. That will give you a few days to get organised. The agency said you've just moved up from somewhere near Manchester. Moving is always a pain. It takes so long to sort things out."

Katy nodded her agreement. You don't know the half of it, she thought.

She left the office in a daze, clutching paperwork to be completed and information about the business. It was only when she'd walked a few metres that she realised she hadn't asked what the job paid and, because it was important for her to be able to budget her money, she returned to ask the question.

"Not what you're used to, I'm afraid," David said. "The wage is sixteen thousand, four hundred a year. Will that be a problem for you?"

"No problem at all, thanks, I just needed to know," she replied and once again turned to leave.

"See you a week on Monday," David said.

"Yes, see you then," she replied happily.

The next day the girls held a party to celebrate. Amongst them they bought a quantity of cheap minced beef, some pasta sauce and dried pasta from 'Saverstore' for the main course. Katy supplied four bottles of 'Lambrusco' to toast her new job, cola for the children and four extra-long, chocolate-marble, cake blocks also from 'Saverstore'. The excitement in the house was palpable. The last celebration was when Emma, a previous tenant of the refuge, was accepted back by her family with the baby they hadn't approved of. The only thing marring the day was that Tricia, on hearing about Katy's job, had been forced to serve her with a four week's notice to quit. With some money in the bank, a new job, and no children to consider, she was no longer seen to be a deserving case for the refuge. However, Tricia had lined up a council-owned flat for her to see that was only fifteen minutes by bus from McLay and Bell's office. She decided that whatever the flat was like she'd accept it. If she hated it, she only had to give one month's notice and it would give her her own space in the short term. When the party was in full swing, she confided in Marie about being asked to leave the refuge.

"Where are you moving to, Hen? Is it close by?" Marie asked.

"I haven't seen it or said I'll take it yet," she replied, "But Tricia said it's in a place called Townhead."

"Aye, Townhead is okay since they rebuilt it. It used to be quite rough but it's okay now and there are two unis and a hospital nearby so lots of students live there. I hope you dinnae mind heights though. There are some low-rise flats but you'll probably be offered one in a high rise. These buildings are over twenty storeys high, but at least they have lifts that work, most of the time, and you'll be close to the buses and trains."

Katy hadn't even visited a high-rise building before let alone stayed in one, but like all the other recent changes in her life, she was sure she could get used to it.

...

Gordon hadn't actually missed, Katy, but he missed her money, her cooking, and he missed sex. In part, he solved the problem of no longer having access to her income by stealing from shops in and around the Manchester area. He also regularly broke into his neighbours' homes while they were at work and took anything of value he could find to sell, making sure he reported a fictitious break-in at his own flat to throw the police off the scent. His meals were supplied courtesy of the local Chinese restaurant or the kebab shop, but for sex, he knew he'd have to make a bit of an effort.

Gordon spruced up himself and the flat as best he could. He even put clean sheets on the bed and sprayed 'Febreze' to mask any lingering odours. He wasn't bad looking and women were often attracted to his cheeky banter. When he'd spoken to Dennis, the landlord of his local pub at the beginning of the week, he'd mentioned that a twenty-strong hen party was booked in for some food and a 'knees up' on Saturday night.

"You might want to keep a safe distance," Dennis said. "The girls have hired a male stripper and it could get pretty rowdy. At the last hen night, the lasses got so drunk, even the taxi drivers wouldn't take them."

Perfect, Gordon thought, just the way I want them, boozed up and turned on. Surely, he'd manage to get one of them to go home with him.

He carefully showered and dressed in his sexiest casual gear, clothes that would show off his muscular frame. He didn't make his way into the pub until after ten o'clock giving the party time to be in full swing. 'The girls' were a mixed bunch, with the youngest being barely old enough to drink and the oldest a woman in her fifties, probably the bride's mother, who clearly felt uncomfortable by the gyrations of the stripper. Gordon spied two women aged in their late thirties or early forties. They were already very drunk, and he watched as one of the women staggered towards the door to get some air. Then he made his move.

He followed the girl to the beer garden at the back of the pub. She tottered slightly on her impossibly high heels, one of which sank into the grass at the side of the path and became stuck. The girl began to giggle as she tried to free herself.

Crouched to her knees she only managed to succeed in sinking her other heel into the grass as well. She was very merry and at the stage of drunkenness when everything amused her.

"Oh dear, what have we here, a fallen angel perhaps? Let me help you sweetheart." The words slid easily off Gordon's tongue. "What's your name? Is it Angelica?"

The girl stared up at him and tried to focus.

"My name's Tracy," she said. "Wow, what big muscles you have. Are you the stripper?"

Gordon flexed his biceps, "All the better to hug you with," he replied.

Tracey laughed and the effort caused her to lose balance, she sat down hard onto the grass and giggled again.

"Please allow me to help you pretty lady," Gordon said flashing his most charming smile.

He stood in front of the girl, grabbed her under the arms and lifted her bodily off the ground. She was very petite, with enormous breasts. He felt a stirring in his loins. Carrying her to one of the tables in the garden, he sat her down while he rescued her shoes which were still stuck in the grass.

"Do I get a kiss for helping you?" he asked.

You can have more than a kiss," she replied. "Bring those muscles over here, big boy. This is meant to be a party, isn't it?"

Gordon couldn't believe his luck. He planted his lips over Tracy's. She tasted of beer and cigarettes, but he didn't care. He embraced her slim frame, holding her firmly with his arm while he expertly reached under her skirt and removed her panties with his other hand. She wriggled slightly and she whispered encouraging words in his ear. She ran her fingers over the muscles on his legs admiringly. Gordon grew hard, his need urgent. He pulled up her body-hugging T-shirt which proclaimed, 'Cara's hen night', hauled down her bra to release her huge breasts then pinched her erect nipples between his thumb and forefinger.

"Ow, not so hard, you're hurting me," she cried, pulling her mouth from his, but he was past the point of no return.

With one arm he lifted her slightly off the table, placed his hard body between her legs and, gripping her buttocks, he roughly entered her. Tracy writhed and whimpered. There was no tenderness in their coupling. Gordon didn't care if she enjoyed the experience or not. After a couple of minutes, she'd had enough of him, but before she could actually ask him to stop, a satisfying throbbing overtook him. He groaned with pleasure as he climaxed. Pushing her away from him, he stepped back. Being full of alcohol-fuelled passion, there was no denying that Tracy had wanted their encounter, but she felt humiliated by Gordon's lack of tenderness. Her eyes filled with tears, and she began to sob.

"I feel sick," she said.

Time for me to go, Gordon thought. Quickly he straightened his clothing and, with Tracy still sitting on the table with her T-shirt pushed up, her bra round her waist and her panties on the ground, he made a quick exit.

That was a cheap night, he thought as he made his way home, and I needn't have bothered changing the sheets.

CHAPTER EIGHT

Once the initial excitement of securing a job was over, Katy knew she had some practical things to take care of before beginning work. Firstly, and most importantly, her wardrobe needed some additions. Although she had enough clothes, she didn't have the correct attire for an office environment. When she thought of all the things she'd left behind, she could have wept. Still, there could be no looking back. She didn't have much money and she'd need every penny when she got a flat, but one suit and borrowed shoes just wouldn't cut it.

"George at ASDA is what you need," Marie said. "The store at Toryglen is open twenty-four hours a day and although their clothes are very cheap, they're stylish. You cannae go wrong with George at ASDA."

"You'll even be able to get shoes and a decent bag there," Lisa said.

"I buy my Brian's school clothes there and if they survive his heavy wear, they'll survive anything," Pat added.

"When the weans are asleep we'll go with you. Nadia can babysit," Marie said. "We can all try on clothes. It'll be fun and we could do with a night out."

Katy wasn't sure that she wanted an entourage to accompany her, but she could hardly refuse when they were being so kind and supportive. She glanced from one girl to the next and was appalled at how scruffy and poor they looked. Then she felt ashamed for judging them. Of course they looked poor, they started off with next to nothing and now they had even less, and yet they'd have given her their last penny to help her. If the shoe was on the other foot, she probably wouldn't have given any of them a second glance never mind a helping hand.

The supermarket was a short bus ride from the refuge. It was huge, bright, and welcoming and surprisingly busy for the time of day. Within the hour Katy had purchased two skirts, two blouses, a pair of shoes and even a lightweight, black suitcase, all for under a hundred pounds. She was particularly pleased with the case as she didn't want to leave the refuge the same way she'd arrived, toting her belongings in a duvet cover.

The group of women laughed and joked as they tried on clothes. They mercilessly teased each other, making remarks like 'mutton dressed as lamb' and 'you look like a stuffed sausage', as they assessed each other's choices. After a couple of hours, they'd tried on everything, bought nothing, and were tired and ready for home.

"We must do this again," Lisa said as they travelled on the bus back to the refuge. "We've had a whole evening of entertainment and it cost us nothing, apart from what Katy needed of course."

"Aye," Marie agreed, "And now Katy dinnae look like a bag lady, carting her belongings about in that terrible duvet cover. What made you buy that ghastly thing in the first place?"

"Yes, it is pretty awful," Pat agreed. "It's just so…"

"Twee," Lisa added.

"I guess my life was twee," Katy replied. "I had the nice job, nice home, lived in a nice area just a shame the husband was a lying, thieving bully."

"They're all the same," Marie said, "Men are bastards, useless, good for nothing, bastards."

But Katy remembered John and the kindness the stranger had shown her. They're not all the same, she thought, and she wondered if she'd ever see him again.

JOHN DIDN'T WANT to offend Patrick. His colleague had been very kind and accommodating and, up until this point in time, he had welcomed his newfound social life. He'd enjoyed the pub quiz, dinner club and games night, but tonight would be different. Tonight was more like a date, and he wasn't sure that he was ready to move on. Particularly as the young lady he was to be paired with was a complete stranger to him. It was all very well for Patrick to say it was just one dinner, but the amount of effort his friend was putting into getting ready clearly showed he hoped it would lead to something more.

John paced the floor. His hands felt clammy with nervous perspiration. He hated sweaty hands and quickly went to the cloakroom to rinse them under the cold tap. He was sure Jenny Archer would be a perfectly nice lady. Patrick had told him she was single, having just ended a two-year-long relationship with a stockbroker, who in his words, didn't want anything meaningful just a bit of eye candy on his arm. Patrick's 'date', Penny Miller had recently been divorced and he was delighted.

"I've fancied Penny for ages," he said when John joined him for a pre-dinner drink. "Her ex was twelve years older than her and very set in his ways. Penny's just thirty-four. She's a long way off middle-age, yet her husband expected her to be happy sitting in front of the telly night after night. I think they're both relieved it's finally over. Do you want a top up?" he asked, proffering the whisky bottle.

John shook his head. "No thanks, I want to keep a clear head, so I don't say anything stupid."

"Calm down, mate. There's nothing to be scared of. The girls won't bite, I wish they would, maybe just a nibble, but they won't, trust me," Patrick said, laughing. "The taxi will be here in about ten minutes, and we'll swing round to Penny's to pick them up."

John shifted nervously from one foot to the other. "I'm not sure I'll be very good company tonight," he said. "I'm not sure I'm ready to date anyone. I lost Carol just under a year ago. I think maybe it's still too soon."

"I keep telling you mate, this isn't a date, just four people who like dining out, eating together. Just like the dinner club, but with a smaller group. We all have to eat tonight and 'Alessandro's' is top rate. We can come home immediately afterwards. It's not as if we're planning on going on to a club or anything like that. It's simply a meal and a bottle or two of good wine."

John nodded. His mouth was too dry to reply.

"There's the cab now," Patrick said. "He just pumped the horn. Drink up and we'll be on our way."

With much trepidation, John walked towards the taxi then got in as Patrick locked the front door.

"Tudor Grove, number four, and don't spare the horses," Patrick said to the driver. "We've got hot dates," he added, winking at John who winced.

"Please don't say that, even in jest," he begged.

"Okay, okay, keep your hair on. No jokes for the rest of the evening."

"Just remember that or you'll be sitting at the table on your own," John warned.

The journey to Penny's house took no more than a couple minutes as she lived only one street away. As soon as the taxi arrived, John jumped out. He stood beside the front passenger door as the girls climbed in, leaving Patrick to sit in the back with them. Once they were all in the cab and on their way, his friend quickly introduced everyone then proceeded to talk about Italian food and the sort of menu they could expect. John was grateful. It broke the ice and there was no requirement for him to add to the conversation. Soon they pulled up outside a very classy looking establishment and he realised that his friend had made a special effort when dressing because of the setting and not just because of the company. John was pleased that he'd also made an effort and chosen to wear his suit, a good shirt, and a tie.

The food and wine were excellent, and the conversation flowed easily. John was very relieved. Under different circumstances he might have been attracted to Jenny as she was just his type, naturally pretty with small even features and a slim figure. Her style of dress was understated, and her manner quite reserved without being dull.

The evening went very well. Although John and Jenny seemed to look on from the sidelines while Patrick and Penny drank a bit too much, laughed a bit too often, and talked a bit too loudly. John was very much aware of being alone. Even in the busy restaurant with good company, he felt alone. When his thoughts turned to Carol there was heaviness like a cold stone in his chest. He made excuses to himself for hanging back, blaming his current situation. Then he thought to himself, what situation? He was single, had been for some time and although Carol was gone, his life was continuing. Somehow after all the pain and loss he was still there, still functioning. It was a sobering thought.

The evening drew to a natural end and before very long they were back in a taxi heading for home.

"We'll drop you off first, Jenny," Patrick suggested. "Because you live furthest away, then we'll go to Penny's. Is that okay with everyone?"

"That suits me fine," she replied, "Sorry to be a party pooper, but unlike the rest of you I'm working tomorrow, and I have an early start, so I'm afraid, that on this occasion, I can't invite you in for a nightcap. It's been a really lovely evening and a pleasure to meet you, John. We'll have to do this again."

Everyone nodded and agreed. John managed to stop himself sighing with relief that Jenny was leaving the group first. There would be no awkward small talk, he thought. She was a lovely girl and very good company. He wouldn't mind becoming her friend, but that was as far as it went.

Within minutes of leaving Jenny's the taxi swung round the corner and pulled in at number four Tudor Grove.

"Home, empty home," Penny said smiling. "The house is so peaceful now that Charles has left. It took him ages to find somewhere he wanted to live so we had to keep sharing the house even though we were separated. Would you boys like to come in for a coffee? You won't have far to walk home. It's handy being just a street apart."

"I hope you don't mind Penny," John said before Patrick could answer, "But I'm really quite tired. I'll take a rain check if I may. Don't let me stop you, mate. I'll take the cab home and I can see you tomorrow."

"If you're sure you don't mind," Patrick said rather too quickly. "I'll see you tomorrow then. Don't wait up, Dad," he added with a wink.

John felt pretty sure that his friend wouldn't be home until morning, but he didn't lock the deadbolt just in case he'd got it wrong. He was very relieved to be back home and alone in his room, comfortable with the solitude.

CHAPTER NINE

When Katy opened her diary the single word 'flat!?' stared back at her. Today's the day, she thought, another new beginning perhaps. She was very apprehensive, actually shaking with nerves, as she made her way downstairs from her room to the hallway to wait for Tricia to arrive.

"Remember, Hen, you can reject this one if it's a shithole," Marie said when she came out of the communal room to offer Katy her support. You can reject the first two and they'll still offer you another so dinnae think you have to agree to take it."

"I hear what you're saying, Marie, but remember my circumstances are a bit different from the rest of you, I don't have children, and because I've been offered a job, I now have means of support. I suppose I'm lucky to be offered anything. I should be at the bottom of the list."

"Still, don't be pushed into accepting if it's nae good," Marie persisted. "You still have rights, you know."

A few minutes later Katy heard Tricia's taxi pull up outside. She quickly gave Marie a hug and said goodbye. Then, as she opened the front door she turned, "Wish me luck. See you later," she said.

"Aye, be lucky, Hen," Marie replied. "We'll still be here when you get back."

When Katy climbed into the cab Tracy was on her mobile and she seemed harassed.

"I've said I'll be over this afternoon. Continually telephoning me makes no difference. I've other calls booked in first. Make yourself a cup of tea and hold tight, I'll see you soon." Tricia rolled her eyes. "A poor wee soul with dementia," she explained as she hung up. "Sorry about that, how are you today?"

"Fine thanks, I'm absolutely fine, a bit apprehensive maybe."

"Don't worry, it's a good building and lots of students live in the area. That always helps."

Katy wasn't exactly sure what it was that the presence of students helped, but she chose not to ask. It took fifteen minutes to get to the apartment block. As they stepped out of the taxi she looked up and up and up.

"How many floors are there?" she asked.

"Twenty-four and we're going to the top," Tricia replied. "We're meeting Bill Martin from the Housing Association at the flat. He's got the keys," she explained.

There was a strong gust of wind. It blew the leaves on the ground into a spiral and lifted them into the air.

"Does the building sway when it's windy," Katy asked nervously. "It looks rather precarious."

"Only a bit," Tricia replied, "Don't worry you'll get used to it, everybody does."

She was about to laugh when to her horror, she realised Tricia wasn't joking. There was an electronic panel on the wall at the entranceway and Tricia pressed the button for the concierge. After stating their purpose, they were buzzed into the building and Katy was relieved to see that the vestibule was clean and bright. Soon they were in one of the three lifts and making their way to the top floor. The lift was equipped with CCTV and, as the doors closed, the confined space smelled distinctly of urine. Katy wrinkled her nose.

"People always pee in lifts in Glasgow, and doorways and phone boxes," Tricia said as if the information would make the habit more acceptable.

Katy was surprised that someone would urinate in the lift when they'd clearly be seen on camera, and she wondered how much effect the concierge actually had. When they alighted at the top floor the door facing them was open and a short, stocky man with a ruddy complexion was waiting to show them inside. Tricia quickly greeted Bill and introduced Katy.

"The old lady who lived here didn't die," he stated. "She's in a home. So don't worry the place isn't haunted," he laughed. "Normally we completely clear a flat of everything even the carpets and we then offer the tenancy for the empty house, but Tricia said you don't have anything of your own, so I haven't actually cleared out the white goods in the kitchen. There's laminate flooring throughout so you'll be all right with that. If you want the white goods, you can have them, but the lease will state that the flat is empty and unfurnished. As far as anyone is concerned the white goods are your own, okay?"

Katy hadn't realised the flat would be unfurnished because she'd never rented from the council before, and it came as quite a shock.

"Thank you, you're very kind," she said. Then turning to Tricia asked, "What will I do about furniture? I have nothing and very little money. At the very least I'll need a bed."

"If you want to take the flat, don't worry, there's a couple of charities that will help. The Salvation Army, for one, either they'll give you what you require, or they'll sell you second-hand furniture at a very cheap price. There's a couple of other charities who'll supply you with starter packs of crockery, cutlery, pots and pans, bedding, all manner of things so don't think about it at the moment, just concentrate on the flat and let us know if you want to take it."

Katy walked over to the large picture window in the lounge and stared out over the city. The view was spectacular. She checked out the bedroom and was relieved to see a wardrobe and shelf unit were built in. The bathroom was fully tiled and had a plain white suite with an electric shower over the bath. The lounge was large enough to hold a sofa and a table and chairs, and the kitchen looked new.

"That's a new kitchen, by the way," Bill said, confirming her opinion. "We only fitted it five months ago. We supplied the new white goods as well, that's why I'm reluctant to throw them away. The bathroom was fitted at the same time. It's a good building. We never have any trouble in this one because the concierge's office is on the ground floor. The block is mostly full of old folk and students, just one or two foreigners and no asylum seekers, they're housed somewhere else."

"You've sold it to me, Bill," Katy replied smiling. "I'm very grateful to you both for all your help. I'd be happy to live here if you'll let me."

"That's settled then," the social worker said. "I'll sort out the paperwork and I'll contact the charities to see what they can give you. We'll try to have you in by Friday. That will give you time to get organised before you start your new job."

As Tricia had to go on to her next appointment, Bill kindly offered to show Katy where the bus stop was so she could catch the bus back to the refuge.

"Don't worry about living so high up," he said as they walked across the estate. "I grew up in a high rise flat in the Gorbals and they were nowhere near as nice as this. In fact, the locals nicknamed the blocks after prisons. Block A was Alcatraz, B was Barlinnie, I lived in Alcatraz on the fourteenth floor. You get used to the height and you get used to the way of life. These flats here in Townhead are the cream of the crop. If they'd been privately built, in this city centre location, you'd have to pay well over £150,000 to buy one of them."

Katy was prepared to take his word for it. For the time being at least she was simply grateful to have a roof over her head. After all, she'd arrived in a new location with very little to her name, so she was delighted with the progress she'd made. Now she had a new job, a new home, and a new life.

CHAPTER TEN

After his liaison with Tracy at the pub, Gordon was complacent. He took risks when stealing and openly tried to sell his loot to traders at the local market. He drank too much, often didn't wash, in fact he was a total mess, so it was little wonder he wasn't lucky with the ladies. He had to blame someone for his lack of success and of course that someone was Katy.

"Everything's fallen apart since my wife left me," he moaned to anyone who'd listen. "Even though she betrayed me I'd have her back in a heartbeat. I love her you see. I've always loved her, and I always will."

It was a load of rubbish, of course, he only loved himself, but it sounded good and sometimes a sympathetic listener would buy him a drink. In reality he was seething. His rage at Katy's flight grew and grew until he could stand it no more. Drunk, and in a fit of temper, he kicked in the glass door of the jeweller's shop in the high street only to pass out on the pavement before he had the chance to steal anything. Then, when the police tried to arrest him, he threw a punch which clipped one of the officers on the chin sending him sprawling. He tried his sob story on the local magistrate, but to no avail.

"You cannot blame your wife for your appalling behaviour," the magistrate said. "This isn't the first time you've been drunk and disorderly, and I'm afraid it's unlikely to be the last. On previous occasions you've been let off with a warning. However, on this occasion, you assaulted a police officer and that cannot go unpunished. I sentence you to two hundred hours of community service. Think yourself lucky that you've been spared a custodial sentence. Do not appear before me again."

Gordon hung his head in mock shame. Silly old fart, he thought. I won't ever appear here again. I'll track down Katy and remind her she's my wife and when I catch up with her, she won't get away from me again. Gordon drank and drank and became drunker and drunker, but through the cloud of alcohol and self pity he hatched a plan.

AFTER AN ENDLESS ROUND of filling out forms, interviews by government officials and charity workers and visits to charity shops, Katy was eventually moved into her flat on Friday. By then she was the proud owner of a nearly new double bed, a pine table with four matching chairs and an old but comfortable sofa. A mishmash of crockery, cutlery, pots and pans, in fact, practically everything she'd need to run a home, arrived in dribs and drabs throughout the day. The elderly lady who was now her neighbour handed in a sieve.

"They never give you a strainer," she explained. "When I first moved in, I couldn't even strain my peas. My name is Mrs. Alison and I'm eighty-two years old. I'm old enough to be most folk's granny, though I don't have children myself. Everyone round here calls me Granny Alison so you can call me that too. The concierge told me you were moving in, so I got an extra steak slice from 'Gregg's'. Come in for your dinner at six o'clock. You never feel like cooking when you first move in because there are always too many other things to deal with."

Katy was touched by the gesture. Steak slice from Gregg's maybe wouldn't have been her first choice for dinner, but the idea of some company and not having to cook appealed to her and it was always a good idea to get to know your neighbours. Granny Alison was slim and strong looking. She had a forceful manner and looked much younger than her years. Katy accepted the kind invitation and thanked the old lady, then she went indoors to organise the flat as well as she could before taking the lift down to the lobby. She'd noticed that near to her apartment block were a handful of shops which included a newsagent and general store, and she made her way there. Within the small line of shops was a launderette, an off-licence, and a bookmaker and all were busy. Surprisingly, for the city centre, surrounding the blocks of flats were grassy areas and in some places play areas for children.

As she walked along the street, she was aware of many young people milling around. Although a handful looked like locals wearing the customary track suits and white trainers, many were better dressed and seemed to be students. These young people gave the whole place a trendier atmosphere and she felt comfortable in their midst. When she reached the shop, she was greeted by a well-spoken Asian girl.

"Just moved in, have you?" the girl asked. "I don't remember seeing you here before. Are you a student? What's your name then? I'm Seher, by the way."

"My name is Katy, and I'm not a student. I have just moved in. I work for an insurance broker."

Seher glanced beyond Katy. "Right, Agnes, hand me that basket and I'll ring your stuff through. We're just gabbing," she said to a plump lady of indeterminate years who was waiting patiently behind her.

As the woman stepped forward, Katy saw she was wearing slippers and she was holding a television remote control.

"If I leave this with ma weans, they'll fight over it and I don't want them breaking ma ornaments while I'm out," she explained.

As Seher rang Agnes' shopping through the till, another couple of shoppers approached the counter. One man simply placed coins in front of her to pay for his paper then left saying nothing. The other held up a packet of tea.

"Ma wife said she'll square up tomorrow if that's okay, lass, she won't trust me with the money in case I buy beer," he explained.

"That's okay, Mr. Costello, tell Eileen I'll see her tomorrow."

Soon the other shoppers had gone and once again she turned to Katy.

"It can be a bit frantic in here, it's lucky we women know how to multitask. Which broker are you working for? I'll probably know them. I'm actually a lawyer you see. When my dad died last year, my wee brother took over the shop. He's in charge of the family now. He's not here because he's taken my sister to Pakistan to meet her future husband's relatives. So, for two weeks, I've been left to look after the shop. Some way to spend your summer holidays, eh?" she added, and she pursed her lips to show her discontent.

"I've just moved to Glasgow. I'm living up there," Katy said pointing to the high rise building in front of the shop. "I'm on the top floor."

"Are you beside Granny Alison then?"

"Yes, that's right. Do you know everyone who lives here?" She was impressed.

"All the regulars," Seher replied. "The students come and go, but some of the old biddies have been here since the flats were built, and I was born here."

Katy glanced at the clock behind the counter. "I'd better pick up my shopping," she said. "Granny Alison has invited me to eat with her and I'm due there in half an hour."

"Let me guess," Seher said laughing, "Steak slice from Gregg's and a wee trifle to follow."

Katy laughed too, "You're right about the steak slice. I'll let you know about the trifle tomorrow."

"Trust me, it will be trifle," the girl replied.

Katy quickly gathered up essentials: bread, milk, cheese, eggs, and such like. On Seher's recommendation she picked up a packet of custard creams and some Typhoo tea for her neighbour.

"That way she won't be out of pocket for your dinner," the girl explained. "She always comes in to buy her tea and biscuits on a Saturday. Granny has her pension counted out to the last penny."

Katy was grateful for the advice as she hadn't considered having to survive on a low budget, but she'd be careful now.

"Have you got everything you need for your flat?" Seher asked as she rang the shopping through the till.

"Most things, but I could do with a television and some books to read otherwise I'll get bored very quickly."

The girl reached under the counter and lifted a paperback book.

"I've just finished reading this. It's set in Glasgow, and it actually mentions Townhead. It's very good, and it grips you. I couldn't put it down. I like reading books based in Glasgow."

She handed over the book which was called, '*The Unravelling of Thomas Malone*'.

"You can borrow it if you'd like. It's about this sad, creepy, young man whose mind slowly unravels. He kills some people and there's a female detective trying to solve the cases. I like crime stories and I found this one really good."

Katy paid for her shopping and thanked Seher for the book.

Before she left the shop the girl said, "I might be able to help you with a telly too. My brother's just ordered one with a forty-eight-inch screen for his bedroom. There's nothing the matter with the old one so when he phones on Sunday, I'll ask him if I can sell it to you. If he says okay, you can have it for fifty pounds. I'll let you know on Monday."

Katy was delighted. She left the shop smiling. If all the neighbours were as friendly as this, she'd be very happy here.

Dinner with Granny Alison proved to be much more enjoyable than Katy could have hoped for. She was very lively and sprightly for a lady in her eighties.

"I was a policewoman until I retired twenty-five years ago," she said. "In my day you walked a beat, so you had to be fit. You can imagine how tough my job was especially in the nineteen fifties and sixties with the Glasgow gangs."

"You still seem pretty fit to me," Katy said.

"That's because I go to the gym three times a week. Old fogies like me get in for free. I have to have an assessment every six months because they're worried in case I drop dead, but so far so good. I don't use any of the heavy equipment, but I like to swim, and I can use the treadmill. As far as health is concerned if you don't use it, you lose it, and I don't feel ready for the knacker's yard just yet."

Seher was right about the trifle for dessert, but she didn't mention the 'wee dram' and mug of tea which was served after the meal. During the evening and with Granny's encouragement, Katy told her neighbour everything that had happened to her. It was a relief to unburden herself and share her story. The two women sat chatting for several hours and Katy was surprised when she looked at the clock above the fireplace and saw it was after midnight.

"I'd better go home and let you get to your bed," she said. "I'm sorry I've kept you up so late. I do hope I haven't over-stayed my welcome."

"I always go to bed late. Old people don't need much sleep

and I've really enjoyed your company. We'll have to do this again."

"I'd love that," Katy replied, "Only next time, I'll cook for you."

When she returned to her home, she locked the door and shut the curtains. It felt good to have her own space and she was amazed how quiet the flat was compared to the noise and hustle and bustle of the refuge. For the first time since arriving in Glasgow she was confident she'd get a good night's sleep.

CHAPTER ELEVEN

*B*y the third week in August and eight weeks into their funding John and Patrick had gathered all the statistics and data they required for their research. All that remained was for them to write up their paper. Each of them was clear which sections they were to handle, and the plan was for them to collaborate once again in three weeks time to collate their work.

August was hot and sticky, and Patrick's modern house felt oppressive. John craved his own home with its thick, red sandstone walls and high ceilings. He actually missed Glasgow with its grimy streets, grey sky, and near constant rain. Even sitting in the garden, if he could have found shade, work was impossible, as the neighbours' children were still off school for the holidays, and they were so noisy he couldn't concentrate. Patrick and Penny had become 'an item' and she seemed to be around all the time. Now that the research work was complete John thought he should go home to do his writing up. It would give his friend his space back and free range to entertain his new girlfriend and John would feel more comfortable both physically and emotionally. He could return at the agreed date for the final collaboration and collation of the paper.

"I hope you don't feel as if I'm forcing you out, mate," Patrick said when John broached the subject.

"Not at all, you've been a perfect host, but I miss my home and my hometown. The Scottish schools are back now and where I live is very quiet. It will be easier for me to concentrate on work as there'll be no distractions."

"Ah, distractions," Patrick pondered. "I'll have to knuckle down when you're away, but Penny is such a distraction."

"If I'm not here you'll be able to work on your own through the day while Penny is in her office then, in the evenings, you'll be able to spend all your time together without me getting in the way. It's the best solution all round. Not that I don't like your company, being here with you has got me back into the world and I'm sincerely grateful."

"It's nice of you to say that. I've enjoyed having a mate to hang out with. We get on so well and I do intend to try to get funding for another project if you're up for it."

"Absolutely, I think we're really onto something and I'd relish the opportunity to take it further."

"While we're on the subject of taking things further, have you any plans to see Jenny again? She likes you. In fact, Penny thinks she's rather sweet on you," Patrick said with a wink.

"All the more reason for me to go home now. She's a nice girl, but I'm not ready for romance."

Over the next twenty-four hours, John purchased his train ticket, said goodbye to people he'd met promising to get in touch again when he returned, and transferred information from Patrick's computer onto his and vice-versa. By the weekend he was on a train northbound to Glasgow.

AFTER A FEW WEEKS Katy was well established in her new job and her new home. With her first month's wages she bought flowers and a bottle of whisky for Granny Alison. She knocked on her neighbour's door and when it was opened, she proffered the gifts.

"Are you sure you can afford this?" Granny asked, her eyes shining with delight. "I'm grateful for the generous gift, you know how much I enjoy a wee dram after my dinner and I haven't had fresh flowers in this house for ages, but I don't want you to leave yourself short."

"It's my pleasure to give this to you. It's just my small way of saying thank you. You've been like a real granny to me these last few weeks, and I can't tell you how much it means to me to have you living next door."

"You've been like a breath of fresh air in this place, Katy. Up until you moved in all my neighbours have been old folk and old folk can be so boring. It's nice to have some young conversation. I know Seher's pleased that you two have become friends. She's a nice lassie and clever like you. I'm just glad her brother hasn't tried to marry her off to some goat farmer in Pakistan. The family enjoy the big money she earns so she's safe for the time being."

"Now, Granny," Katy scolded, "You know her sister is going to marry an accountant not a goat farmer and it's someone she met at university here in Glasgow. His family live in Pakistan, but he has a big house in Newton Mearns. I'm sure Nusrat will be very happy."

"We'll see," the old lady conceded. "She'll probably end up a bored housewife with five children instead of being an optician as she was trained to be. What's the point of all that work to get a degree when all she'll end up being is a housewife and mother?"

"Trust me Granny, if I could be a housewife and mother instead of working full-time and being on my own, I'd be delighted. I'm about to consult Seher about getting a divorce so I can move on, but I'd love to meet someone decent to spend my life with."

"Well, I guess what you've never had you never miss. I personally loved being in the police and my life was very fulfilling. Everybody's different I suppose. Anyway, thank you once again for your very generous gift. Would you like to come for dinner tomorrow? It's Friday and I could get some steak slices from Greggs and a couple of wee trifles. We could have a double measure with our tea," she said, grinning and holding aloft the whisky bottle.

"Thanks, that sounds great. I've just bought a fruit cake, so I'll bring in a couple of slices to have with the tea."

With the arrangement made both women returned to their homes and Katy felt really happy. Mentioning to her neighbour about seeking a divorce somehow made it feel real and she was eager to meet up with Seher to set things in motion. The sooner she was free from Gordon, the better.

***

Gordon had dreamt up his plan weeks before, but it wasn't until now he had the means to go forward. It was a chance meeting in the local supermarket that gave him the information he required. He recognised Betty, the receptionist from Katy's former job, immediately, and he quickly engaged her in conversation.

"I was so sorry to hear about the break-up," Betty said. "How are things now?"

"Great, Betty, really great," he lied. "I've got a new job and I'm earning good money now. Katy will be able to stop work and we can start a family. That's all she's ever wanted, but when I was out of work the pressure was awful."

The lies rolled off his tongue easily and seamlessly, one after another.

"So, is she coming back from Glasgow, then?" Betty asked.

"Yes, she's just got to work her notice at...sorry I can't remember the name of the company she's working for."

"McLay and Bell," Betty offered.

"Yes, that's it, McLay and Bell."

Got you, Gordon thought. McLay and Bell in Glasgow, you can run but you can't hide.

"I'm delighted for you both," Betty said. "I always thought you were the ideal couple."

"Thank you, Betty. I'm sure Katy will call you when she gets back."

Gordon practically skipped home. In another few weeks he'd complete his community service then he'd pay Katy a visit. He'd soon sweet talk her into coming back home and this time he'd never let her leave.

CHAPTER TWELVE

Within a few weeks Katy had settled easily into her new position and her new home. As predicted by the women at the refuge, after she left, she made no contact with any of them. She was delighted to be able to put the refuge and the part of her life it represented firmly behind her. Her workplace was friendly, and she had an easy rapport with the people employed there. On the last Friday of every month the boss treated his staff by buying everyone a cream cake to have with their coffees and special events like birthdays were celebrated in the same way. The business generated enough work to keep everyone busy so all in all the days were free from pressure because everyone's job was assured.

Katy's home life was comfortable too. She spent time with Seher who'd become more than just an acquaintance. The two young women often went out together, visiting the high street shops most Saturdays and the cinema every Wednesday evening when they could get two seats for the price of one. Dinner with Granny Alison had become a weekly event, so she wasn't lonely.

It was the last Saturday in October, and the girls were having coffee in Starbucks in the city centre. Seher explained to Katy that because she and Gordon had been married at Gretna Green, a romantic whim which seemed ironic now, she could get divorced in Scotland so there would be no need for her to travel back down south.

"I can simply arrange for him to be served the papers then it's up to Gordon to sort himself out. He's never tried to get in touch with you so the whole thing will probably just amble along until it completes. I don't suppose he'll contest the divorce," Seher said.

"I'm not so sure," Katy replied. "He always has to win, he's very competitive and he hates to lose at anything. He always has to be in control. I think the only reason he hasn't been in touch is because he doesn't know where I am. To tell you the truth, I could have gone anywhere. I bought a ticket on the first train out of town, and I didn't have a clue when I arrived at the station, where I was going or what I was going to do. A kind man on the train helped me. He even gave me his card so I could get in touch with him because he was trying to find me somewhere to live. He was the one who took me to the hotel in his taxi. My head was in a mess, and I was distraught. I arrived in a strange town at night, knowing nobody."

"Why didn't you contact him? Was he a bit of a sleaze? Did he frighten you?"

"No, quite the reverse, he was a perfect gentleman. I wanted to get in touch with him, but when I was rushed into hospital in the early hours of the morning, his card was lost. The hotel packed up my belongings and delivered them to me, but the card wasn't amongst them. They probably threw it out when they cleaned the room without realising it was important to me."

"Couldn't you try to trace him, maybe through Facebook or something like that? What was his name?"

"John, he told me his name was John Houston and he was a lecturer, some kind of science, I think."

"A lecturer should be easy enough to find. Which university?"

"I'm not sure," Katy replied. "But it's too late now anyway. I don't suppose he'd be interested in hearing from a complete stranger. What could I say? The flat he was going to help me with will be gone now and I'm perfectly happy where I am."

"A handsome, kind stranger helps you in your time of need. He has a good job, and you like him, of course you should try to find him. I take it he's single, you did establish that didn't you?"

"He's a widower. He told me his wife died about a year ago and he missed her enormously. They were childhood sweethearts."

"Yeah, yeah," Seher replied dismissively, "But she's gone now and after a year he'll be ready to move on."

"You're impossible, you do know that. The poor man was heartbroken."

"I'm sorry, Katy, but life goes on and you're about to file for divorce. You don't want to let a good catch slip through the net. Trust me, there's not too many of them around."

"I hear what you're saying, but I have no intention of phoning a virtual stranger to thank him for being kind to me, not after all this time. I've missed the chance, it's over. If I tried to get in touch now, he'd think I was some kind of crazy stalker."

"It might be better than turning into some sad old spinster like Granny Alison," Seher added determined to have the last word.

...

As arranged, John briefly returned to Patrick's, and they completed their work. Both men were delighted with the result and excitedly spoke of working together in the future. They enjoyed each other's company and knew that their friendship would last far beyond their working relationship. The anniversary of Carol's death came and went while John was in Manchester, and he was pleased to have the distraction of his work. He didn't mention the date to anyone, so the day passed by like any other, but of course it wasn't. The weight of his loss was as heavy as it had ever been, but he was learning, little by little, to live with it.

When he returned to his home once again, the house felt cavernous. The emptiness of each room hung over him like a dark cloak and the space he once thought of as his sanctuary, felt like a prison. He had to get out in the air, had to breathe. He craved company and began to accept invitations, any invitations, anything to be out in the world. His grief at being alone turned to anger. Why did his Carol have to die? She'd never hurt a soul in her life. Why did he have to suffer this awful loneliness? In his heart he knew the anger he felt was simply the next stage in the grieving process and common sense told him he'd get through it, but it was difficult. He needed distractions.

The autumn evenings were mellow and warm, and John began to drive down to the coast several times a week. He liked to walk along the shore and listen to the waves and the gulls cry as they soared overhead in the updrafts. He met lots of people walking their dogs and, had his life been different, he too would have acquired a dog for company. As things were, it would have been unfair to keep an animal shut in most of the day while he was working.

Friends and family started inviting him round for meals and social evenings. He had become the extra man that one invited when faced with an odd number at the dinner table. Over the previous weeks he'd found himself paired with the single cousin, sister, or friend of just about everyone he knew.

"Sir, I'd be honoured if you'd come to my home on Saturday

evening. We're going to celebrate the completion of my research. As my esteemed tutor, you will be one of the most important guests. My wife is a very good cook, and all our close friends are coming."

The invitation came from Khalid Ali, one of John's students who'd popped into his office near the end of the day. John was surprised and touched by the request. He'd tutored Khalid and mentored him and now the young man was to be awarded a doctorate. He felt Khalid easily deserved the accolade. He'd been a model student and researcher and he'd worked tirelessly. His wife Sadia was a doctor working at the Royal Hospital while her husband studied. John respected the couple. He'd only briefly met Sadia, but he knew Khalid well and enjoyed the young man's company.

"How kind of you to invite me," he replied. "Is it a formal dinner? Will I have to give a speech? I'm not very eloquent," he joked.

"So, you will come," Khalid said, and he breathed a sigh of relief. "I'm so pleased, sir. My mother is attending, and she really wanted to meet you. My father will be coming over from Pakistan when I am to be presented with my degree, but he can't leave his business at this time, so you will be representing him at my party. I'm delighted you will be there, sir. Without your assistance I would not be celebrating. You have helped me so much."

The enormity of the honour wasn't lost on John, and now he was worried that he would indeed have to give a speech.

"It will not be a sit-down dinner, more of a buffet, but the food will be good, I promise you that, sir," Khalid continued. "My wife is one of those fine ladies who are not only clever, but also great homemakers. She never stops telling me what a lucky man I am to be married to her," he added, smiling at his own joke. "The evening will begin at six o'clock and you know, of course, we do not serve alcohol."

Khalid gave John the address and he saw that the young man lived in an area called Townhead which was beside the Royal Hospital.

"Sometimes Sadia has to work nights," Khalid explained. "The flat we rent is just a few minutes walk from the hospital. It's not an upmarket area. Where I live in Pakistan is very superior, but Townhead serves us well."

"I'll see you at six on Saturday then," John replied. "And don't worry, I won't let you down. I'll tell your mum you were a model student, and I'll sing your praises in my speech, even if I have to toast your good health with apple juice."

"Trust me, sir," he replied. "My health is better for being toasted with apple juice. Have you seen some of the people in this city? They get so drunk they fall down in the street."

John couldn't agree with him more. Nevertheless, he thought, he'd better have a couple of drinks before arriving at the event to give him some Dutch courage and he'd better write a speech.

CHAPTER THIRTEEN

Katy and Seher met at McDonalds early on Wednesday evening. The weather had changed from mellow and warm to damp and there was a distinct chill in the air. The girls had opted for the fast-food restaurant because the film they wanted to see was screening earlier than their previous choices. Each had come straight from work, and each had stories to tell.

As they stood in the queue to order Seher began, "We had a client in the office today called Mr Woodcock. Christine, the secretary, and I had to sit in on the meeting and she kept whispering rude jokes to me about his name. That wasn't helped by my boss having a slight speech impediment and pausing between the words 'wood' and 'cock'. I was terrified I'd laugh out loud and embarrass myself."

"We have clients called Heather Feather and Hazel Nutt," Katy said. "These are their chosen names, not names they've gained through marriage. Imagine their parents knowingly saddling them with those names."

"Yes, what can I get you?" a skinny young man behind the counter asked interrupting their chat.

"Sweet chilli crispy chicken wrap, fries, and a coke," Katy replied.

"And I'll have a spicy veggie sandwich, fries, and an Irn-Bru," Seher added.

The fast food was indeed fast and soon both girls were sitting at a table wolfing down their meals.

"I want you to come to a sort of party with me on Saturday night," Seher said. "It's just a finger food buffet at my friend's flat in Townhead. She lives in Glebe Court just a couple of minutes from you. Her husband has completed his doctorate and they're celebrating. His mum's coming over from Pakistan and Sadia wants some moral support because practically everyone else at the party will be Khalid's friends and work mates. I don't want to go on my own. Please say you'll come."

"I'm happy to come with you, but I don't know the protocol. What should I wear? Should I take a gift, perhaps flowers or a bottle of wine?"

"Wear whatever you like as long as it's not too bare. We don't want to shock his mum. You don't need to take anything because I'll have a gift, but if you feel you want to, take flowers or shortbread biscuits, something like that. Definitely don't take alcohol. They're all Moslems like me so they don't have booze in the house."

"What time do you want me to be ready?"

"I'll call round for you at five-thirty. The evening kicks off early, at six o'clock. Talking about time, we'd better get going, the film programme starts in fifteen minutes and we've still to buy tickets."

"Don't worry the adverts last about twenty minutes so we've plenty of time," Katy said. "Let's get a McFlurry to eat while we walk to the cinema. I fancy ice-cream with Smarties what about you?"

Seher opted for a Cadbury Crème Egg McFlurry and the girls ate as they walked and talked. The Cineworld cinema complex was in the very heart of the city. At twelve storeys high it is the world's tallest cinema. The journey up and up on the escalators to reach their floor seemed endless, but even so, Katy marvelled at the eighteen-screen facility. She loved coming here. The screens went from wall to wall and from floor to ceiling and the acoustics were amazing. It didn't take the girls long to become engrossed in their movie and enjoy the whole Hollywood experience.

Although they found themselves back on the street at only nine o'clock both girls were tired and neither had been home yet after work.

"The film was great," Seher said, "I loved the clothes and the setting."

"And the servants," Katy added. "Maybe one day I'll be rich."

"You'd better come into our shop and buy a lottery ticket then, the winning lottery ticket, because I don't see either of us having that sort of money any other way," her friend replied.

"After my divorce from Gordon I might marry a millionaire," Katy speculated.

"Oh yes, and where are you going to meet this amazingly wealthy man? Maybe he'll be strolling in Townhead or eating at McDonalds or perhaps he'll come into your office to see your boss about insuring his pet."

"You're just a killjoy, a rotten killjoy, for all you know my millionaire might have been sitting at the next table."

Seher guffawed with laughter. "A smelly old down and out was sitting at a nearby table, then there was the group of spotty teenagers wearing track suits or maybe the millionaire was the dodgy looking guy covered in tattoos. Dream on girl, dream on."

...

Gordon leant on the brush he was supposed to be sweeping the site with. Only another five weeks of this awful work, he thought. He'd be finished his community service in five weeks then he'd be free. By mid-December he'd never need to look at

Mr. Barker's ugly face again. He hated the smug bastard with his constant stream of one-sided views about crime and punishment. Of all the people he could have been assigned to Mr. Barker was probably the most annoying. The other lads made jokes about never committing a crime again just to avoid him. Gordon, on the other hand, just wouldn't get caught the next time. He'd make sure of that. He'd rob enough people and accumulate enough money so he could travel to Glasgow and fetch Katy home. Assuming of course he didn't lose his tenancy first. The amount of unpaid rent due was increasing, and he'd have to pay the landlord something soon or face eviction.

He knew he'd have to do everything in his power to sweet talk her into coming back with him. He'd be the ideal, remorseful husband. He'd agree with everything she said, constantly apologise and assure her he'd never raise his hand to her again, anything in fact, just to get her back.

There'd be time enough to sort her out once they were back together and she belonged to him once again. He'd really suffered since Katy ran away. How dare she abandon him, she'd promised to love him and more importantly, obey him. He'd make her pay for all the misery she'd caused. He'd make her pay.

WHEN KATY LAY in her bed that night she daydreamed about her millionaire. He would be clever and kind and understanding. He'd love her and cherish her and sweep her away on his white charger or perhaps in his Rolls Royce or his yacht. Her millionaire would never shout or lose his temper. He'd never raise his hand to her. The man of her dreams would be a passionate but tender lover. They'd have a family and live in a big house with a garden, and they'd entertain friends. Seher and Granny Alison would visit her beautiful home and she'd cook wonderful food for them, and Granny could have a double measure of whisky with her tea every night.

Katy felt comfortable and cosy in her bed. Her dreams warmed her heart and filled her with hope. The man in her dreams was always handsome. He always had kind eyes and, for some reason, when she pictured his face, the man of her dreams was always John, the stranger from the train.

CHAPTER FOURTEEN

John arrived at the ground floor flat in Glebe Court at ten past six. He didn't want to be late, but neither did he want to be the first to arrive. The security door was open, wedged with a piece of paving slab, so he entered the communal hallway, located Khalid's door, and pressed the bell. The hallway floor was washed and smelled distinctly of bleach and the flowery scent of air freshener hung in the air. He heard footsteps from inside the flat coming towards him, and there was a fumbling of locks then the door was pulled open. When Khalid saw him, his face lit up, and he grinned from ear to ear. He reached out, grabbed his hand, and pumped it vigorously.

"Professor Houston, you're here, my esteemed mentor, you are here," he said his eyes filling up with emotion.

As John was led down the narrow hall, he could hear voices and laughter coming from a room towards the back. The two men entered the lounge, and he was surprised to see several of his fellow lecturers and some of his students standing in small groups chatting.

"The women are in the kitchen preparing food and talking. They'll join us shortly," Khalid said.

That explained why there were no women in this room, John thought.

"Yes, Professor, the men talk in one room and the women in another. That's the only way we men can get a word in edgeways," a young man with a shock of red hair joked, offering his hand for John to shake. "Remember me?" he asked, "I was in your lectures last year.

"Of course, I remember you, Craig," John replied smiling. "You consistently turned up late, fell asleep in my lectures, yet somehow you still managed to get a first-class degree. How are you? What are you doing now?"

"Actually, I'm lecturing in Paisley, and I have this one lad who consistently turns up late, who falls asleep in my lectures and will probably get a first-class degree. He irritates the hell out of me. You'll be pleased to hear that what goes around comes around. Sorry I was such an ass, Professor."

The two men exchanged laughter. John continued to mingle and, before very long, he had another dinner invitation and had been asked to attend a pub quiz with a group of students.

"We really need you, Prof," one of the young men said. "We need someone with a knowledge of cheesy nineties music and we're all too young."

"Yeah," another chipped in, "We missed out on a crate of beer last week because none of us knew who sang '*Barbie Girl*' or '*Cotton Eye Joe*'. Do you know, Prof?"

"'*Barbie Girl*' was performed by 'Aqua', '*Cotton Eye Joe*' by 'Rednex'," John replied, surprised by his own knowledge.

"See," the first young man said full of admiration. "I told you lot the Prof would know. He's an old guy. We need an old guy on our team."

"Just a minute there, Sonny Jim, who are you calling old? I'll have you know I'm still in my thirties."

"To us that's old," the young man replied. "My folks are in their thirties, just," he added. "Anyway, you're smart, and we need you. What do you say?"

Somehow John found himself part of the group and agreed to attend a quiz at a city centre pub on the evening of the following Tuesday. As well as cheesy nineties music he was assigned tv programmes from the same era to read up on.

"Is everything okay, sir? The food is just coming. The women will put it on the table by the window where paper plates and cutlery are already laid out. Everyone has to help themselves. Can I get you a drink, sir? Perhaps, apple juice?" Khalid asked with a smile and John knew he would soon have to deliver a speech.

KATY AND SEHER rang the doorbell at ten to six and they were the first to arrive, but within five minutes the kitchen held eight women. Fortunately, the space was large.

"Women always try to arrive a few minutes early to help the hostess lay out the food," Seher explained. "Any earlier, and she'll still be preparing it. Any later, and she'd have done all the work herself."

The girls were introduced to Sadia's mother-in-law as soon as they arrived.

"My name is Ayesha but call me Auntie," the older lady instructed.

"It's a term of endearment," Sadia explained out of earshot of Ayesha, "Quite common in Pakistan for mothers-in-law, although I call her Mummy. She's very kind to me, but very bossy. I'm so glad you could come Seher and you too Katy. She's been telling me how to do this and how to do that all afternoon. I'm a doctor, for goodness' sake. I think I'm capable of preparing some pakora and samosas. Anyway, I've got to keep my cool for

Khalid's sake. She's staying with us for two weeks you know. I'm glad I'll be at work most of the time. Khalid can entertain his mother."

Katy and Seher exchanged knowing glances.

"She sounds stressed already, and her mother-in-law has only just arrived," Seher whispered. "Can you imagine how she'll be after a fortnight?"

"What are you girls muttering about? Come over here to me. Put the chicken on that tray Seher and carry it into the room where the men are. They must all be starving. This food should have been out ten minutes ago."

"Yes Auntie," Seher replied obediently. "At once, Auntie," she said, and she giggled as she carried plates of food through the adjoining door into the lounge.

The women continued loading plates while Seher carried them to the buffet table. Katy enjoyed the easy banter in the kitchen. The camaraderie made her feel like part of a family, and she enjoyed the interaction with the other women. Soon all the food was in place and the women went through to the lounge to join the men.

Ayesha was led over to the front of the room and introduced to the gathering then Khalid explained to everyone, that as his father couldn't be with them, his esteemed professor would be giving a speech on his behalf. Everyone applauded as John was introduced, everyone except Katy who froze on the spot.

"How could you do this to me, Seher?" she hissed at her friend. "How could you bring me knowing he would be here? You could have warned me. At the very least you could have warned me. This is so embarrassing. I suppose you thought you were doing me a good turn, but you're not. I told you it was too late to get in touch with him. I told you."

Seher was mystified. She had no idea what her friend was talking about.

"What are you talking about?" she asked. "Who is here? I've done nothing. Why are you upset?"

"John," Katy replied with exasperation, "The stranger from the train. That's him, standing next to Khalid about to make a speech."

"Oh, my goodness, are you sure?" her friend replied. "Are you absolutely sure it's him? What a coincidence."

"Coincidence, you mean you didn't get in touch with him."

"Of course not, how could I have? This is Khalid's party. John is his friend."

After her initial shock at seeing him, Katy knew Seher was telling the truth. She stood quietly behind her friend with her head bowed, planning what to say to John when he finished his speech. Part of her was thrilled at the prospect of meeting him again, but part of her was terrified and embarrassed because she hadn't got in touch before.

"If you'd rather leave, you could sneak out as soon as he finishes his speech. I'll apologise to Sadia and tell her you weren't feeling well," Seher offered.

"Thanks, but I'll talk to him and explain what happened. I couldn't help being ill and it was bad luck that I lost his card. I didn't purposely ignore his kind offer."

"He's good looking, very good looking in a preppy, intelligent sort of way," Seher whispered.

"Shh, people will hear you. Wait until his speech is over to talk," Katy chided.

John's speech was funny and flattering. He sang Khalid's praises, complimented his wife and his mother then he took a small box from his pocket.

"This is a gift to remind you of all the time and effort you put into gaining your doctorate," he said.

Khalid opened the box to reveal a silver-plated card case.

"You'll need new business cards showing the name Doctor

Khalid Ali," John explained. "Now you'll have something to carry them in. If I could ask everyone to be upstanding and raise your glasses," he continued, "To Doctor Khalid Ali," he toasted.

"To Doctor Khalid Ali," the assembly echoed.

Everyone began chatting again. "It's now or never," Katy said to her friend and biting her lip she made her way over to John.

Although he was talking to someone, he excused himself when he saw her approaching.

"Hello," he said shyly. "I never thought I'd see you again. How are you?"

Katy smiled, "Better than a couple of minutes ago. I was nervous about coming over to talk to you. You must think I'm awful, letting you help me then not getting in touch, but I can explain if you'll let me."

"Why don't we sit over there?" he replied, "The small sofa is free and it's in the corner, so we won't be overheard."

They sat down and Katy told him everything that had happened to her. Once again, the kind stranger listened without interruption. After speaking for over half an hour she apologised.

"I'm so sorry you must be bored to death. It's bad enough that you had to listen to all my troubles on the train now I'm telling you another round of 'what Katy did'."

"Please don't apologise," he replied. "I'm delighted to be in your company. I'm just sorry you've had such a terrible time. I'm especially sorry about the baby. What did your husband say?"

"He never knew I was pregnant, and I intend to keep it that way. I've filed for divorce, and I don't want to complicate things. I just want to be free to get on with my life."

"So, are you socialising? Have you made many friends? Do you know the Alis because you live beside them?"

"No, I didn't know them at all until this evening. My friend

Seher, the girl standing beside Sadia, brought me along tonight, but in answer to your question, I am socialising, but I don't know many people."

"I see, I see," John said. He looked thoughtful. "I've started to go out again. It's been a year since Carol died and I feel ready to join the world again. I've been going out to dinner and to pub quizzes, that sort of thing."

"I go to the cinema with Seher every Wednesday, and I eat dinner with my elderly neighbour once a week, nothing as exciting as a pub quiz," Katy joked.

John held his chin in his hand. They sat in silence for a moment before he said, "I might be completely out of line here and please, shoot me down if I am, but would you like to come to a pub quiz on Tuesday? A group of students have asked me to join their team. We could have some pub grub and a drink. These quizzes usually don't go on very late and the pub isn't very far from here. I'd see you home afterwards. They're only asking me because, in their words, I'm an old guy who knows old stuff."

"Good grief, what age are they if they think you're old? They must be children." she replied laughing.

"Some of them are still teenagers, so I guess they are. One of them even told me I was the same age as his folks."

John and Katy talked and talked and gradually the room emptied as people went home.

Eventually Seher approached them and said, "Sorry to interrupt, but it's getting late, and I have a busy day tomorrow. I'll need to leave in a few minutes."

"Sorry, Seher," Katy replied standing up from the sofa. "Doesn't time fly when you're enjoying yourself? Let me introduce John and John this is my very good friend, Seher."

After they shook hands Seher went to fetch their jackets while Katy said goodbye. She wrote down her address for John so he could collect her for the quiz on Tuesday then after thanking their hosts the two girls left.

When they were a distance from the flat Katy said excitedly, "I've got a date. Just for pub grub and a quiz. Oh, and we'll be joining some students, but still, I've got a date and I have you to thank for it."

CHAPTER FIFTEEN

hen John got home, he poured himself a large scotch. He was excited about meeting up with Katy, but he couldn't help feeling guilty. Carol's photograph stared at him from the mantelpiece in the lounge. Her sweet mouth smiled, and her bright eyes sparkled. How could he possibly go out with another woman? He drank his whisky then poured himself another. He knew in his heart that Carol wouldn't want him to shut himself away. She had loved him and always wanted the best for him. It was cruel and unfair that she'd died, leaving him lonely and alone.

He looked around the room which was full of things they'd chosen together. Carol would always be part of his life, but she was gone now, and somehow, he had to carry on. Every time he looked at her photograph he cried, but he could no longer wallow in his misery, it was self-indulgent and pitiful. He had to allow himself to move forward. Carefully, he lifted down the photograph. "Goodnight my darling," he said. Kissing the glass, he slid the photo into the drawer of the sideboard. Gently he pushed the drawer closed. He could look at it whenever he wanted, but the time had come for him to rejoin the world, he was ready to climb out of his dark place and move forward. He was ready to stop feeling sorry for himself and live again.

KATY WAS EXCITED about meeting John. Their conversation had flowed easily and naturally. She felt safe and relaxed in his company, and she realised now that she hadn't felt this way with Gordon for a very long time. In fact, she wondered if she'd ever been relaxed in his company. He'd always told her what to do, how to dress, what to think. She'd thought it was because he loved her and wanted to protect her. To be the strong man she could rely on to look after her, but she now realised that he had always been a bully, a spoilt man who had to have everything his way or no way.

As she lay in her second-hand bed in her little council flat on the top floor of the high-rise building, she felt content. She had fewer material things and a less demanding job than before, but she was content. Everything she had was hers and hers alone. Every choice she made was her decision uninfluenced by anyone else. She had real friends who cared about her unconditionally. Katy hoped that Seher was right, and Gordon would simply accept that it was time for them both to move on. She was ready to step out of her dark place, a place where she was often on edge, fearful of his rules and his temper. She was ready to move forward and live again.

TUESDAY EVENING DULY ARRIVED, and John felt like a nervous teenager as he stood outside Katy's building. He'd dressed carefully, remembering that everyone he was meeting up with was younger than him. He wore jeans, of course, as they were considered 'de rigueur' for the venue, topped with a plain black T-shirt and jerkin-style jacket. All were new, bought the previous day in 'Top Man', as he didn't trust anything in his wardrobe to be suitable. The young, male shop assistant who advised him was about the same age as the lads in the quiz team, so John trusted his judgement over his own.

Taking a deep, calming breath he pressed the number on the security pad and waited for Katy to answer. After a couple of moments, he heard her voice.

"Hello, who is it?"

"Hi, it's me, John. Are you ready or will I come up?"

"Give me a minute and I'll come down, I'm ready, I just have to lock up. I'll press the button to let you into the foyer."

There was a low buzzing sound and the door slid silently open. He entered and paced the floor nervously looking from lift to lift for signs of one of them descending. Within a minute the one on the right began coming down and the panel lit up as it passed each floor. The doors slid open and there she stood, looking even more beautiful than he'd remembered. Like him, Katy was wearing jeans, but hers were topped by a pretty blue blouse which perfectly accentuated the colour of her eyes.

"I wasn't sure what to wear," she said. "Is this alright?"

"Beautiful," John replied. He couldn't take his eyes off her. For a moment there was an awkward silence then he cleared his throat. "You look beautiful and very appropriate for the venue."

"I have to admit, I wasn't sure, so I went into Top Shop and asked an assistant," Katy said. "I'm a bit out of touch when it comes to choosing what to wear to a pub."

John burst out laughing, "Me too," he said then he pointed to his clothes. "T-shirt, jeans and jacket, all from Top Man, I was nervous in case I looked too much like a boring old fart, so I went into the shop and asked a young lad for advice."

The laughter broke the ice, and both were relieved. As they made their way out of the building and walked towards the pub, Katy slipped her arm through his. This action felt natural, and they walked in step, chatting about work, likes and dislikes, anything that came to mind.

The pub was in the heart of the city, and it was unlike anything Katy had ever seen before. It was very large and lively, full of people shouting to each other above the loud music that was booming out of speakers which seemed to be everywhere. It was so noisy she could hardly hear John speak. Surely they couldn't hold a pub quiz here she thought? They fought their way to the bar where John managed to get the attention of one of the barmen.

"Is there a quiz being held here tonight?" he asked. "I was told you held one on a Tuesday."

"Up those stairs, pal, in the tapas bar," the man answered, pointing to a spiral stairway to the right of the door. "There's a big money prize tonight as well as a crate of beer. It's a rollover, two hundred pounds. Good luck, pal. Can I get you anything just now?"

John looked at Katy.

"Let's wait until we're upstairs," she answered. "I don't fancy trying to carry a drink through this crowd."

He thanked the barman then, holding Katy's elbow, they negotiated their way through the crowd and climbed the stairs. They emerged into a large quiet room set out with long trestle tables and a bar at one end. John spotted the quiz team immediately.

"Over here, Prof," one of the young men stood up and called to him. When they joined the group the young man, who was called Liam said, "I'm so glad you could manage because two of the team have cancelled. We thought we'd be down to just the four of us."

John quickly introduced Katy to the group which consisted of three boys and one girl. The other boys were Paul and Gary. Liam introduced the girl as Chas and said she was his sister. John always thought Chas was short for Charles, but he didn't risk asking any questions because she looked more butch than the boys. She had a skinhead haircut, tattoos, piercings and muscles a wrestler would have been proud of.

John got in the first round of drinks, and Katy was commandeered into the team to make up the numbers. They ordered some tapas from the bar and the group were in fine spirits when the quiz master duly appeared. Their group was called the 'Bar Flies' and, after several rounds of questions, they found themselves in tied first place with another group aptly named 'The Blues Brothers' as each member wore a dark suit, hat, and shades.

"The tie break question is going to be on the books of Jane Austen," the quizmaster said.

There was a simultaneous groan from the 'Blues Brothers' and the 'Bar Flies'.

"We don't know anything about Jane Austen," Liam said morosely. He looked miserable.

"You speak for yourself," Katy piped up. "I've read all her books at least twice and I've seen several films and TV productions. I'm a sad old romantic, you see," she explained.

Everyone grinned. "There's a crate of beer at stake and two hundred pounds," Chas said. "That's over thirty pounds each," she stressed.

"And the question is," the quizmaster said then made a drum roll with his hands on the table. "What was the name of the first Jane Austen novel to be completed for publication?"

Once again the 'Blues Brothers' groaned in unison.

"I know, I know, tough question, but it is a tie break and it's worth two hundred quid and a crate of beer."

The 'Bar Flies' looked expectantly at Katy.

"It's not really about the content of her books. It's not really a fair question," Paul moaned.

Katy smiled, wrote something down on the quiz form and

slid it across to Liam, their team captain. "I agree with you Paul, but I know the answer," she said, grinning.

Her teammates gave a loud whoop, and Liam rushed forward with the paper.

The quiz master looked at the sheet then said, "And the answer is '*Northanger Abbey*', and the winners are the 'Bar Flies'. Congratulations."

The group at the table erupted with stamping feet, cheers, and whistles. John grabbed Katy and planted a kiss on her lips followed by everyone else in the team patting her on the back and kissing her cheek. The group was ecstatic. After receiving their prize and dividing the loot, Katy and John said goodbye to the others and headed back towards Townhead. Both agreed it was the best night out they'd had in a long time, and they were already planning another date. When they reached her building John accompanied Katy to her front door.

"I'm so pleased we met again," she said as she stood in the doorway. "I've had a great time."

"Me too," John agreed. "I'll call you tomorrow after work. Would you like to have dinner with me on Thursday? I know you see your friend on Wednesdays."

"Thanks, I'd like that."

They stood awkwardly for a moment as each was unsure what to do next. Finally, John plucked up the courage to embrace Katy. He gently pressed his lips to hers and the touch was electric. His heart pounded in his chest, his lips trembled slightly, and he felt a passionate stirring in his loins. He drew back. He didn't want to be too full on, not at this early stage in their relationship.

"I'm sorry," he said, unsure what he was apologising for.

"Don't be," she replied breathlessly, and she drew him back for another embrace.

John held Katy close as his mouth found hers once again. Their kiss was fierce and passionate, their lips and tongues searching, probing. Even after the kiss had ended, they clung to each other, reluctant to part.

"I'd better go," he said with a sigh.

She nodded. She knew the time wasn't right for anything more, but she wanted more.

"Until tomorrow then," he said.

"Yes, we'll talk then, until tomorrow," she agreed. But as John got back into the lift and Katy entered her flat and shut her front door behind her, she added, "Tomorrow, and tomorrow and tomorrow."

CHAPTER SIXTEEN

"Well, tell me what happened," Seher said. "I want to know every last detail. Did he kiss you? Did you ask him back for coffee? Did you…you know?"

"Yes, he kissed me. He walked me to my door, but didn't come in and no, of course we didn't. It was our first date for goodness' sake," Katy replied.

"Ah, so it was definitely a date then. Are you seeing him again?"

"He said he'd call today so get off the phone. He might be trying to get through. I'll be seeing you in twenty minutes for the cinema and we can talk then."

"I'm coming round. I'll be there in ten, I've just got to do my hair," Seher replied.

Katy was about to say don't come round so early because she wanted to be able to have a private conversation with John when he phoned, but before she could say another word, she found herself listening to the dialling tone. The minute she placed the phone back on the table it rang again, and her heart skipped a beat. It's him she thought as she answered.

"Hello Katy, remember me? I'm the guy who's been awake

all night thinking about you."

She smiled, "Hello John," she replied softly.

"Did you have a good day at work? Do you still want to go out to dinner with me tomorrow? Do you fancy Italian food?"

"Yes, yes, and yes," Katy replied then she said, "Seher is about to appear here at any moment, so you'll understand if I can't talk. She's so nosey, but she has my best interests at heart."

"Yes, she seems like a lovely girl and, from what you've told me, a good friend. Why don't we arrange for me to meet you after work tomorrow then we can go straight out? There's a great little restaurant on the south side, just ten minutes from your office, it seems a shame for you to travel all the way into the city centre then have to travel back again."

"That sounds like a plan. What's the place like?"

"Small, intimate, up-market casual, the food is superb, and the atmosphere is great. I think you'll like it."

Katy heard the buzz from the security phone.

"Sorry, John, but that's Seher buzzing up. I'd better go," she said as she pressed the button to let her friend into the building. "I finish at five but by the time I'm ready to leave it's usually nearer ten past."

"I'll be waiting for you when you come out. I'm really looking forward to seeing you again."

"Me too," she replied.

They ended their phone call just as Seher rang the bell.

"Well, did he call?" she asked when Katy opened the door.

"Yes," Katy replied as she stepped aside to let her friend enter the apartment.

"And? Are you going on another date?"

"Yes, we are."

"Well tell me about it, when and where? Goodness it's like trying to pull teeth getting information out of you. I want to know everything."

JOHN WAS EXCITED about the date he'd arranged. He couldn't help smiling whenever he thought about it. Suddenly, after months of putting off the task, he decided the time had come to put his house in order. Armed with black bin sacks and steely determination he began to clear things out, beginning with the wardrobe in his bedroom and, more specifically, Carol's side of the wardrobe. Several months before he'd managed to bag most of her clothes and donate them to charity, but there were still some items that he hadn't been able to bear parting with. Personal things that stirred memories of the good times they'd spent together. Her wedding dress for one and the sun hat she wore on their honeymoon in the Seychelles. Many, many items, far too many, his home had become a shrine, but it was time to move on. He would of course have his photographs, Carol's wedding ring, and the heart shaped pendant he'd given her when they'd first started to date, but the soft toys they'd won at the carnival, ornaments, and an assortment of knick-knacks would have to go.

Once he started, he worked like a madman. Sweat poured from him as he went from one room to the next, packing and bagging all manner of things. When he finally finished it was nearly one o'clock in the morning. The house looked bare and minimalist. To John it seemed empty, but he knew that the rooms were clean and fresh, the house was elegant and stylish and, more importantly, he would now feel able to invite people in. He'd shut himself away, hiding like a small creature in its burrow, but now, at last, he could breathe.

OVER THE NEXT two weeks John and Katy went on several dates and by week three they couldn't get enough of each others' company. John was romantic and kind. He bought Katy flowers and when they visited the theatre, a small box of hand-made chocolates to nibble on during the show. He wined her, dined her, and wooed her. After much soul-searching, he now felt ready to move the relationship forward and, with that in mind, he made up the double bed in the second bedroom with new, crisp, Egyptian cotton sheets. He didn't want to bring someone to the bed he'd shared with Carol, and he vowed to replace it and redecorate the room as soon as possible. John filled the bedroom with flowers, hoping Katy felt as he did. He would never push her to do anything she was uncomfortable with, but when they kissed and embraced her passion was as intense as his, and when he held her in his arms, he could feel her body tremble with desire. It became more and more difficult for him to leave her at the end of the evening, but he didn't want to rush things. He wanted their relationship to be something special, something lasting.

Although it was Saturday, Katy cancelled her usual shopping day with Seher as she wanted to spend the time pampering herself for her evening with John. She was dining at his home for the first time, and he was cooking for her. No man had ever cooked for her before, and she was charmed. She hoped this evening would take their relationship forward and with that in mind, she carefully packed fresh underwear, a toothbrush, and her make-up into her handbag. Fortunately, big bags were in fashion so having one didn't make it look as if she was expecting to stay over. If the opportunity didn't arise, if the time wasn't right then he need never know she'd come prepared.

Katy lay in her rose-scented, bubble bath. She'd already laid out on the bed the clothes she'd be wearing, a decision that had taken nearly an hour. Even though she didn't own many clothes, she'd tried on every piece in her wardrobe, in every possible combination, before finally settling on a fine-wool, figure-hugging sweater dress. She liked the feel of the soft wool on her skin. She imagined John touching the fabric as it clung to her body, and she became breathless with desire at the very thought of spending the night with him. He was everything she could possibly wish for in a man. Katy wanted him and prayed he felt the same way about her, but she didn't want to rush things. She wanted their relationship to be something special, something lasting.

When John arrived to collect her, Katy was waiting at the doorway of the building. She was a vision of loveliness, perfect in every way. He marvelled that this beautiful, younger woman was attracted to him. They had a lot in common and the more they dated the more they realised that they liked and appreciated the same things. As she walked towards the car, he leapt out to greet her and open the door.

"You look absolutely stunning," he said.

Katy found herself blushing.

"You look pretty good, yourself," she replied.

As they drove through the town towards the south side, tenement properties gave way to the stylish houses of the suburbs. When they pulled up outside John's house, Katy was surprised.

"Does the entire house belong to you or is it divided into flats when you step inside?" she asked.

"It's all mine and it's a devil of a job to clean," he joked. "The house is far too big for one person, but that's not what I'd planned when I bought it."

There was an awkward silence for a moment.

"Anyway," he said, opening the door, "We'd better get inside so I can check on the dinner. I don't want to give you a burnt offering."

The house looked even bigger on the inside and Katy was rather overwhelmed by the opulence of the place. However, within a few minutes John had opened champagne and soon they were sitting at the dining table, eating and chatting as if it was the most natural thing in the word.

The food was delicious, expertly presented and the wine was a robust, red burgundy. When they'd finished eating, at John's suggestion, they moved to the oversized, white leather sofa in the lounge. He placed his arm round Katy's shoulders. She turned to him, and they kissed, deeply and passionately. Her body tingled with desire. She slid her hand along the length of his muscular leg. He gently caressed her, letting his hand linger on her breast. The soft wool clung to her slender body, his need for her heightened until he could hardly bear it.

"I want you," he gasped. "If you want me to stop, tell me now."

"Don't stop, I want you to make love to me," she replied.

John stood, took Katy by the hand, and led her to the room he'd prepared. Silently they undressed one another then they climbed between the cool sheets. He was tender. He selflessly and gently caressed her, kissing her neck and her breasts, holding back his lust until she could bear it no more. She pulled him to her.

"Please, I want you now, I want you," she gasped.

They kissed deeply and passionately holding back nothing. They writhed, their legs and arms entangled, moving together as one until Katy felt wave after wave of passion overcome her. Seconds later she felt John climax and a satisfied moan escaped from his lips.

Katy lay contentedly in John's arms.

"I've never felt like that before," she said. "Gordon never cared about my needs."

"Gordon was a fool. He didn't deserve you, but he's out of your life now. I'll never hurt you," John said, and Katy believed him.

She felt her eyes fill with tears of emotion, "I think I'm falling in love with you," she whispered.

CHAPTER SEVENTEEN

Gordon received the divorce papers the same day his community service ended, and he was enraged. Bitch, he thought, stupid bitch, she can't divorce me. I won't let her. Katy's going to be my meal ticket for the rest of my life she just doesn't know it yet. He hurled his coffee mug at the kitchen floor where it shattered, sending jagged shards all over the room. Stupid bitch, just wait until I find her and tell her how it's going to be, she'll soon get the message.

He grabbed his rucksack and filled it with his best items of clothing. He placed a box of stolen jewellery in a side pocket of the bag and stuffed all the money he could find into his jacket pocket. Finally, he put the divorce papers into the bag and zipped it closed.

"No time like the present," he said aloud as he left the flat, slamming the door behind him.

He didn't bother locking up because it was about to be repossessed and anyway, he'd sold anything of value, even items of furniture belonging to the landlord. He'd meet up with Katy, win her over and they'd have a fresh start. Gordon had heard that Glasgow was a vibrant city and now he'd find out if that was true.

KATY WAS ON CLOUD NINE. She was so happy she was fit to burst. Seher had arranged for the divorce papers to be served on Gordon and she knew he'd received them as they'd been signed for. It was simply a waiting game now while their lawyers sorted everything out. Seher was confident he wouldn't contest the divorce because as they'd lived in a rented flat and they hadn't any savings to speak of, there was no joint property to sort out. And as he never had any money, it was unlikely he'd travel to Glasgow. Katy was worried about him finding out where she lived, but her friend assured her that in cases of domestic abuse the address is kept private. The refuge had encouraged her to file a police report about the abuse as soon as she'd arrived, and she was pleased that she had because it added strength to her position.

She and John were like two love-struck teenagers. They were always seeing each other, thinking about each other, or speaking on the phone. Katy couldn't quite believe how much her life had changed.

NOVEMBER SAW the shops full of Christmas goods and John loved it. He wanted to be jolly this festive season now that he had someone to share it with. He and Katy had already decided to invite Granny Alison and Seher for a celebration lunch at his home and, as Seher didn't drink alcohol, she offered to save John the journey of collecting the old lady. Instead, she would bring her then return her to her home later in the day. John felt joyful, he even found himself humming Christmas carols. Every day at lunchtime he searched the shops for the perfect gift for Katy. He would buy her the moon and the stars if he could.

That evening he'd arranged to spend only an hour at her flat because he had to attend a faculty meeting at the university at eight. They would just have time for some fish and chips then he'd have to leave. Still even an hour was better than no time at all. When she arrived home, he'd already collected the food and was keeping it warm in the oven. They'd now exchanged keys to each other's homes, and it made things so much easier.

"I'm sorry I have to shoot off," he said when they were seated at the table. "At least we'll both be free tomorrow. I miss you so much when we're apart."

Katy nodded. "I feel as if we've always been together. We've become so close."

They quickly ate their food then Katy stood up, took John by the hand, and led him to the bedroom.

"I can't be late for this thing tonight," he said, but even as he spoke, he knew his protest was half-hearted.

They made love with intensity each relishing the joy of their coupling.

"I don't want to leave you," John said.

"But you must," Katy replied. "You said yourself you can't miss this meeting."

Someone had to be the voice of common sense. After they'd dressed, Katy walked John to the lift. Once again, they kissed passionately holding each other close. When the lift arrived, she eased herself from his arms.

"Go now before I change my mind," she said.

He blew her a kiss as the doors slid shut.

"See you tomorrow," she called.

WHEN GORDON ARRIVED IN GLASGOW, he booked into a hostel for two nights because that was all he could afford. Yesterday he'd located Katy's place of work and when she'd finished for the day, he'd followed her home. It wasn't too difficult to get into the building as at that time of the day people were frequently coming and going. He'd seen her enter the lift and travel to the top floor, so he knew where she lived. Now he was back.

He waited until nearly eight o'clock to be sure that she was in for the night before taking the lift to her floor. Finding the correct apartment was easy because there was only one without a nameplate and none of the others bore her name. Gordon straightened his clothes, fixed his best smile on his face then rang the bell.

John must have forgotten something Katy thought, and she hurried to open the door. She was shocked to the core when she saw Gordon standing in front of her and she tried to push the door closed, but he was too strong.

"Don't shut me out," he said, forcing his way into the flat. "I've come all this way to see you."

He looked about him at the clean, tidy space then the smile left his face, and his expression became thunderous. Katy was frightened.

"Get out of my flat," she shouted. "I want you to leave now. If you don't get out, I'll call the police."

"And by the time they get here, it will be too late," he replied menacingly. "Why don't you just be nice to me? How about a kiss for your long-lost husband?"

She was really scared and tried to back away, but he grabbed her arm and pulled her to him. She turned her head as he tried to kiss her. His hands were all over her body and she felt sick.

"Let me go, get away from me," she screamed trying to wriggle free.

Gordon threw her onto the floor. He took the divorce papers from his jacket pocket and waved them in front of her.

"I'm still your husband," he shouted, "And I still have rights."

Katy was terrified. She began to scream.

He laughed, "That won't do you any good," he said.

Granny Alison was startled. At first, she thought it was the television she was hearing, but when Katy began to scream Granny knew she was in trouble. Through the wall she could hear a man's voice. He sounded angry and he had an English accent.

"Oh, my God," she said aloud.

Without hesitating she reached for the phone and dialled 999. Quickly she told the police what was happening. Then she hung up and called Colin, the concierge, to ask for assistance.

"Hurry," she said. "Please, hurry, I'm frightened he'll kill her."

Granny searched her kitchen drawer, and, in a moment, she'd located a key to Katy's flat. She'd had the key for twenty years after being given it by her friend Enid, who'd been the previous tenant. She'd forgotten about it until now. With the key in one hand and her whisky bottle in the other she raced out of her flat and across the hall. The whisky bottle was the only heavy item she could find. In her police days she used a baton to tackle thugs, but the bottle would have to do. Granny used her key and was relieved to find the lock hadn't been changed, normally it would have been, but given the circumstances of the outgoing tenant and the speed with which Katy had moved in, it had been overlooked.

With no thought for her own safety, she entered the flat, leaving the door open for Colin and the police. Then she followed the sounds to the kitchen in time to see Katy cowering on the floor and Gordon raising his hand to strike her. A rapidly blackening bruise on Katy's cheekbone was evidence that he'd hit her already.

Granny stepped forward and brought the bottle down on Gordon's wrist. It made a satisfying crack. He doubled over in pain and cried out.

"What the hell," was all he managed to say before she swung the bottle again, smashing it against his knee.

Katy scampered across the floor on all fours. She grabbed Granny by the arm and dragging the old lady with her, made her way to the front door. The two women burst into the hallway just as the lift door opened and Colin stepped out. The second lift opened a moment later and two policemen emerged. Gordon was roaring and swearing. He limped through the doorway only to be wrestled to the ground by the police.

"I'm the victim here," he screamed. "That mad old woman broke my wrist and smashed my knee."

"Is that true, Granny? Did you break his wrist?" the older policeman asked with a smile. All the police officers knew Granny Alison in this area. She was a legend in her own time.

"It was self-defence," she stated stubbornly. "He attacked my friend in her own home, and he would have attacked me too if I hadn't defended myself."

"Once a cop always a cop," the officer said, his voice full of admiration.

"I want to press charges for assault," Gordon spluttered. "I've a right to be here, she's my wife," he said, nodding towards Katy.

"He forced his way in," Katy said. "He beat me."

"Why don't we all go back inside and see if we can't sort this out," the older cop said. "From what I can see, you're in serious trouble, sir. You could get years inside for attacking a woman in her own home and causing actual bodily harm, and as for threatening an elderly lady, well, who knows, they might throw away the key."

"That old bat broke my wrist," Gordon protested.

"That sweet old lady is over eighty years old," the cop replied.

They all entered the flat. Katy was shaking with shock. Quickly she explained about the abuse and the divorce papers and before very long the policeman gave Gordon an ultimatum.

"If you want to avoid serious charges, sir," he said, "You will sign these divorce papers for your wife. I'll witness your signature. Afterwards, my colleague and I will drive you to your hostel to collect your belongings and we'll put you on the first train heading south. Then you'll never appear in this jurisdiction again. Do I make myself clear?"

"I can't get a train. I don't have money for a ticket," Gordon sneered. "I don't have any money since she left me."

"I'll give him the money," Katy offered, "Anything to be rid of him."

Before very long the policemen left, taking Gordon with them.

"I can't thank you enough, Granny," Katy said. "You saved my life."

"Never underestimate the power of a mad old woman," her neighbour replied laughing. "It's lucky I work out at the gym."

Granny stayed with Katy until they both calmed down then the two women turned in for the night. Katy lay in her bed clutching the divorce papers in her hand. She was battered and bruised but she was free.

CHAPTER EIGHTEEN

During the next few weeks Katy and John grew closer and closer. From a chance meeting on a train, she had found the love of her life and he discovered that happiness can return if you open your heart.

Christmas came with a flurry of snow. As Katy lay in the comfortable, king-sized bed that she and John had chosen together she heard him moving about downstairs. She could hear the sounds of him working in the kitchen. He wanted this Christmas to be special for her. He wanted to look after her, cherish her. Her heart melted at the thought of him rising at the crack of dawn to toil in the kitchen preparing the food for their Christmas lunch while she slept. He treated her like a princess, and she loved him for it. She stretched lazily and was about to get out of bed when she heard John coming upstairs. He entered the bedroom carrying a tray.

"Good morning, Darling. Merry Christmas," he said. "The turkey's in the oven and everything else is in hand. I've made us breakfast," he added, placing the tray on the bed.

"I love you," Katy replied, "Merry Christmas you lovely man."

They kissed tenderly then John reached into his pocket and produced a small box.

"I love you too," he said.

John opened the box and Katy's heart skipped a beat.

"Is this what I think it is?" she asked softly.

She stared at the beautiful engagement ring. Catching the light, the diamond sparkled almost as brightly as her smile.

"I know we'll have to wait a while, but will you marry me and make me the happiest man in the world?" he asked.

"Yes, John, I will," she replied, sighing contentedly. "I've waited my whole life for you."

Once again, they kissed tenderly. John slipped the ring onto Katy's finger.

"I'll love you for the rest of my life," he said, and she knew that what he said was true.

"You are my life," she replied.

And, as the snow fell silently on the ground outside, John and Katy gazed happily into each other's eyes as they planned their future together.

END

ABOUT THE AUTHOR

Hi, my name is Elly Grant and I like to kill people. I use a variety of methods. Some I drop from a great height, others I drown, but I've nothing against suffocation, stabbing, poisoning, or simply battering a person to death. As long as it grabs my readers' attention, I'm satisfied.

I've written several novels and short stories. My series 'Death in the Pyrenees' comprises, 'Palm Trees in the Pyrenees,' 'Grass Grows in the Pyrenees,' 'Red Light in the Pyrenees,' 'Dead End in the Pyrenees,' 'Deadly degrees in the Pyrenees' and 'Hanging Around in the Pyrenees.' They are all set in a small town in France.

'The Unravelling of Thomas Malone' as well as a collaboration of short stories called 'Twists and Turns'.

As I live much of my life in a small French town in the Eastern Pyrenees, I get inspiration from the way of life and the colourful characters I come across. I don't have to search very hard to find things to write about and living in the most prolific wine producing region in France makes the task so much more delightful.

Perhaps you will visit my town one day. Perhaps you will sit near me in a café or return my smile as I walk past you in the street. Perhaps you will hold my interest for a while, and maybe, just maybe, you will be my next victim. But don't concern yourself too much, because, at least for the time being, I always manage to confine my murderous ways to paper.

Read books from the 'Death in the Pyrenees' series, enter my small French town, and meet some of the people who live there ----- and die there.

Alternatively read about life on some of the toughest streets in Glasgow or for something more varied delve into my short stories.

To learn more about Elly Grant and discover more Next Chapter authors, visit our website at www.nextchapter.pub.

ALSO BY ELLY GRANT

Death in the Pyrenees Series:

Palm Trees in the Pyrenees

Grass Grows in the Pyrenees

Red Light in the Pyrenees

Dead End in the Pyrenees

Deadly Degrees in the Pyrenees

Hanging Around in the Pyrenees

Angela Murphy Series:

The Unravelling of Thomas Malone

The Coming of the Lord

Death at Presley Park

One Dark Year

Twists and Turns (short story compilation with Zach Abrams)

But Billy Can't Fly – an irreverent black comedy (co-authored with
Angi Fox)

Never Ever Leave Me
ISBN: 978-4-82412-285-8

Published by
Next Chapter
1-60-20 Minami-Otsuka
170-0005 Toshima-Ku, Tokyo
+818035793528

10th January 2022